Walter Chalmers Smith

Raban: or, Life-splinters

Walter Chalmers Smith

Raban: or, Life-splinters

ISBN/EAN: 9783337056315

Printed in Europe, USA, Canada, Australia, Japan

Cover: Foto ©Andreas Hilbeck / pixelio.de

More available books at **www.hansebooks.com**

RABAN:

OR,

LIFE-SPLINTERS.

BY

WALTER C. SMITH.

Glasgow:

JAMES MACLEHOSE,

PUBLISHER TO THE UNIVERSITY.

1881.

Inscribed

To the Memory of

My Wife,

My Stay and Solace and Inspiration.

Eheu!

CONTENTS.

Endings.

Stray Leaves.

Raban.

When first I knew him, Raban was already
Verging on age, yet full of lusty life;
With all his senses perfect to enjoy
The fatness and the sweetness of the earth,
And all its beauty; and with all his mind
Perfect to do its work—to reason well,
To play with graceful fancy, or mirthful jest
That rushed from him, like spark from glowing steel,
I' the clash of argument: and he could soar
Still into realms of thought that touch the stars,
And lie about the Eternal; and his heart
Was very young, and nothing loved so much
As the fresh hopes of noble-purposed youth
Not yet desponding of a glorious world.

A

Trim and erect, with locks of iron-grey,
A large eye full of light, and features thin
That grew with age in beauty; a manner brisk
And breezy; ready of speech for sharp retort,
Or flowing period; given to dainty humour,
Where delicate touches of quaint character
Flitted like smiles upon his words; he knew
Affairs and books and men, and it was like
Great music just to sit beside the fire,
And hearken his discourse.
                                        One of a race,
Often much slighted, often serving much,
Who miss their aim in the first spring, and fall,
A season, out of sight among the waste
Of prodigal life; yet better so kept back
In the young bud, than in the bloom of promise
To be frost-bitten, for he found a way,
And filled a larger space by having failed
Than first success had given him. He had once
Sought the Priest's office, well content to be
The humble pastor of a humble flock
Of shepherds 'mong green hills, or of dull hinds
Whose thoughts are of the mixen or the calves,
Hard to lift Heavenward. But he was not made
For the Priest's work, whose Sundays domineer
The week with preaching, as he goes about

Slow sermon-grinding till his thought is thin
As the shrill fife, the while he makes his rounds,
And hears the parish-gossip, and grows small
With its small interests, only, now and then,
Lit up by broader lights that shoot athwart
From that dread door which opens for all men.

Orthodox? Well; I think he had not any
Cut-and-dry scheme—equation nicely framed
With *plus* and *minus* quantities and powers,
Subtracting or dividing human sins
By sorrows of the Highest, till the end
Brought out salvation neatly. Somehow he
Could never work the problem out so clear,
Having an Infinite quantity to deal with,
That would not balance with a sum of littles,
However multiplied. Therefore he had
No handy formulas for faith, and shunned
Familiar phrase of preaching, which he called
Old pulpit-dust beat from the cushion when
Thought is most lacking; also he would try
Perilous flights, at times, into far realms
Of fine imagination, where his flock
Followed him only with their eyes, as one
Watches a cloud soar up, and fade away
Into the setting sun.

             And yet his faith
Was true to the old Creeds he left behind,
As the fresh art of a new age still holds
All past achievement in its scheme of progress,
And moves on the old lines. He kept their spirit ;
Only the framework, and the rigid joinings
Clamped, as with iron, by mistaken texts,
He loosened ; for he deemed the truth was there,
But yet in forms too rounded to be true,
And clothed as with an armour which grew not,
Though the man grew within, till what was meant
For a defence, brought weakness. Thus, at times,
He seemed to assail their most secure beliefs,
And sap the main foundation of their hopes,
When he was merely setting free the soul
Of Truth, on which they lived, and which he loved ;
Only they knew it not without the husk,
Nor could they live on it without the straw,
Which they were used to, while he would refine,
And from all gross admixture purify,
Till he could sip it like an odorous dew.

So have I heard him tell that, by and by,
No flock would eat his pasture ; where he came
They wandered off to sit beside the fire,
Or saunter in the fields considering

The lilies how they grew, or to rehearse
Questions once learnt beside a mother's knee,
And pray for the old gospel of their youth.
"And they were right," he said; "man cannot live
Without his formulas—I was a fool!
Your disembodied, unfamiliar thought,
Like disembodied spirit, frightens him;
Or he seems left, as naked in the cold
And dark, amid the crash of breaking ice,
And polar fogs wherein he sees no light,
But the ice-glimmer everywhere. And yet
'Tis well for you to-day that I was left
To play the fool; I think ye have more light
That I lie in the shade; your life is larger
That mine was straitened—freer through my bonds."

I found among his papers sundry traces
Of that old time, when he was preaching faith
Just as he learned it, day by day, and oft
Erasing one day what he writ the last
Upon their puzzled minds; a hint or two
Of hope and failure, and some things he called
"Crystallized sermon," tied up with a string.

So he forsook the priesthood, trying first
Scholastic tasks, and in his leisure hours

Penning brief essays, quaintly humorous
Or thoughtful, with the flavour of a soul
Fresh from the vision of a dewy world
That still seemed very good : and people noted
The promise in them of an unknown power.
Ere long the breakfast table mirthful grew
With an incisive and sarcastic wit
That played about our cloudy politics
With ridicule like reason ; now and then,
Unfolding, too, new depths of social right,
And hopes for men that staggered the dull brain
Of rural squires believing in their game,
And rural priests believing in their teinds,
And burghers cushioned in old customs good
For people well-to-do, but quickened life
And expectation in the poor oppressed.
Soon this man grew, by writing and by speech,
A power among us ; unto some he seemed
A Firebrand fain to set the world ablaze,
Class against class, and all against the Faith
Which anchored men to God by prophet-forms,
Where prophet-vision was not : but to some
He brought the hope of better days a-coming,
And brighter future for their dismal life.

But when I knew him, he had dropt his pen,

And done his work, and took his well-earned leisure
Cheerfully, as a man who had not lived
In vain ; but could look back upon a path
Troubled with battle and turmoil, hope and fear,
And frequent disappointment and defeat,
Yet brightened, too, by trophies of success—
By growth of right, of freedom, and of knowledge,
And power to grow still more, wherein he had
No little part. Now, round his restful years
Honour and love were gathered ; gratitude
Grew out of service lightly once esteemed,
But in its full achievement plainly seen
To fruit with good for all. A happy lot
Wisely to serve your day, and in the glow
Of evening feel its calm steal over you,
And see the people glad, and hear them sing
Of the ill times you helped to better for them.

I met him, first, when hunting for a book
Among the stalls where he was hunting too,
Now his life's chiefest business, and its joy :
And I, being fearful that he sought the same
Rare volume, looked askance at him, and weighed
My scanty purse with his, doubtful ; till he
Who knew book-hunting minds, and slender means,
Saluted me, and we grew friends ere long,

Having a common love of curious lore.
Thus meeting, by and by, I found my way
Into his home, which once had been made bright
By a fair helpmate, and by joyous girls
Lightsome as flowers : but it was lonely now,
And silent, for they all had gone before
Into the silent land. I found his rooms
All lined with books, and littered too with books
On chair and table and floor; pale-vellumed classics—
Sound English calf, respectable—grey-paper
German, soon dog-eared—French like buttercups—
Aldine editions costly, beautiful—
A Caxton—tiny Elzevirs—and Scotch
Imprints at Capmahoun—tall copies scarce—
Fair tomes emitted by the press beloved
Of him who, praising Folly, smote the monk,
And grinned out of his hood : books everywhere,—
Folio and quarto, duodecimo,—
Luxurious editions—titles quaint
With curious woodcuts—travels, stories, poems ;
All precious rubbish that a Book-worm loves ;
And there I revelled—who so happy as I ?
What joyous hours we had there as he showed
How this was precious for a curious blunder,
That for an autograph, one for a comma
Oddly misplaced, another for its margin,

Its Type, its Title, or its Colophon!
Skilled in this lore, he yet laughed at his skill,
And passed a thousand jests upon a taste
So foolish, while he fondled some loved prize,
Quarto or folio, like a babe beloved,
And told the story of its search and capture,
And how he brought it home like one who walked
Among the stars, and sang for very joy.

We grew close friends, for all his friends were young,
And that which linked him with the Past, his love
Of ancient lore, was less than that which drew
His heart to the opening Future; full of hope
He hung about the dawn, like morning star,
And watched the coming day; not fearing greatly,
Although he saw the germs of larger change,
And deeper movements in the thoughts of man
Wrestling for birth, than centuries had known.
But falling sick, at length, he slowly sank
Beneath a wasting ill that broke his strength,
Yet not his spirit, for he still was gay,
And grimly jested at his racking cough,
Made merry with his bones that fleshless grew,
Cheating the worms, he said; and under all
Lay a great calm of Faith and surest Hope.

One evening, sitting, lonely by the fire
A letter came to me, black-bordered, sealed
With skull and cross-bones, yet his writing plain.
I opened it in fear, and there I read

The Letter.

I begged hard for an hour of grace
    From that grim Ferryman who plies
His wherry to the fore-doomed place
    Of all the foolish and all the wise.
But not an hour the churl will give,
    Nor deigns to answer me, though I,
Who always was in haste to live,
    Would rather take my time to die.

Another sun, and I shall know
    The secret Death has kept so well:
What wonders in a day or so
    A letter writ by me could tell!
And yet who knows? I've mostly found
    That secrets are but sorry stuff;
And those that lie beneath the ground
    Perchance are commonplace enough.

I've lived my life; it has not been
    What once I hoped, nor what I feared;
And why should that we have not seen
    Be other than has yet appeared?
There are no breaks in God's large plan,
    But simple growth from less to more;
And each to-morrow brings to man
    But what lay in the day before.

The river has its cataract,
    And yet the waters down below
Soon gather from the foam, compact,
    And just like those above it flow:
And so the new life may begin
    Where this one stopt, with finer powers,
Perhaps, the subtle thread to spin,
    And years to work instead of hours.

What has my life been that my heart
    Should be so tranquil at this time,
So free to ply the careless art
    Of guessing, and of tagging rhyme?
Here on this solemn brink of doom
    I seem not much to fear or care,
But peer into the gathering gloom,
    And mostly wonder what is there.

And that has been my bane all through,
   That never yet would life appear
So real that my hand must do
   Its work with earnestness and fear:
Still I could dream and speculate,
   And turn it somehow into play,
And nothing woke a perfect hate,
   Or love that had its perfect way.

I tried the highest life—and failed;
   A lower, with a small success;
I loved; I sorrowed; laughed and railed
   At Fortune and her fickleness;
And powers I might have trained to grow
   I frittered, for I was not wise;
And now their fire is burning low,
   Their smoke is bitter in the eyes.

Ah! wasted gifts and trifling gains!
   Ah! life that by the abysses played,
And partly knew the griefs and pains
   That from the depths their moaning made,
And partly felt them too, and yet
   Could be content to dream and write,
Or in old story to forget,
   And never wrought with all thy might!

You'll find in an odd drawer the sum
  Of that life, rich in nought but friends—
A grasshopper's dry-throated hum,
  A hank of broken odds and ends;
Do with it as you will; I give
  My all to you; perchance it may
Beacon another soul to live,
  More wisely through its changeful day.

You'll pay my debts—they are not large;
  You'll bury me where the poor folk sleep;
And for the rest, my only charge
  Is that the dear old books you'll keep.
If ghosts come back, mine will be met
  Upon the steps among the shelves,
Searching for mildew, moth, or wet
  In the small quarto's or the twelves.

And now farewell, my lad; fear God,
  And keep your faith whole, if you can,
And where the devil has smoothed your road,
  Keep to the right like an honest man;
See that your heart is pure and just,
  See that your way is clean and true;
By and by we shall all be dust,
  Yet by and by I shall meet with you.

The world is losing faith in God,
   And thereby losing faith in man,
For now the earthworm and the sod
   Wind up, they say, our little span;
But they that hold by the Divine,
   Clasp too the Human in their faith,
And with immortal hopes entwine
   The silence and the gloom of death.

I read, and, hastening to the house, I found
'Twas even as he said. In his last hours
He wrote, and gave strict orders not to send
The letter till his final breath was drawn,
And now he lay there mystic, beautiful.

Never, in all those years, had I once dreamed
That he, in secret, plied the Poet's art.
He flaunted in the face the hardest facts,
Brought reasons by the score, had strokes of wit
When reasons failed, and bubbled o'er with fun;
But never passing word, or tremulous tone,
Hinted of Love's sweet sorrow, or of song
Long brooding o'er the tragic bliss o' the heart;
'Till now I found these lyrics scattered, most,
Loose in a drawer, and cast them into shape
As I could trace the thread: and gathered up

The broken fragments with the care of love,
That nothing might be lost of a true life.
For he that truly lives, and clearly sees
The truth wrapt in his life, and can set forth,
Amid the trivial and the commonplace,
The soul of truth for which he dared to live,
Leaves to the world a nobler legacy
Than wealth of hoarded gold, in that he kindles
Lights on the dim, uncertain way we go.

Preludes.

B

Dreaming.

I dream beside that silent sea
  Which yet has mystic voices low
That whisper potent words to me
  From the dim, haunted long ago;
And as the waves, with measured beat,
Drift up the slow wrack to my feet,
Faces gaze from it, sad and sweet.

So come they, as the stars appear
  Even while you gaze on the blank night;
For ere you wis, lo! far and near
  The dusk is all agleam with light;
A mighty host, uncalled, they come,
And without sound of trump or drum,
But yet their silence is not dumb.

They speak to me of hopes and fears
That yet can make my bosom thrill,
As o'er the weary waste of years
The dead hands reach, and touch me still
For that old Past still lives to me ;
Its phantom faces still I see,
More life-like than the living be.

Work and Spirit.

Is it the work that makes life great and true?
  Or the true soul that, working as it can,
Does faithfully the task it has to do,
  And keepeth faith alike with God and man?

Ah! well; the work is something; the same gold
  Or brass is fashioned now into a coin,
Now into fairest chalice that shall hold
  To panting lips the sacramental wine:

Here the same marble forms a cattle-trough
  For brutes by the wayside to quench their thirst,
And there a god emerges from the rough
  Unshapely block—yet they were twins at first.

One pool of metal in the melting pot
  A sordid, or a sacred thought inspires;
And of twin marbles from the quarry brought
  One serves the earth, one glows with altar-fires.

There's something in high purpose of the soul
  To do the highest service to its kind ;
There's something in the art that can unroll
  Secrets of beauty shaping in the mind.

Yet he who takes the lower room, and tries
  To make his cattle-trough with honest heart,
And could not frame the god with gleaming eyes,
  As nobly plays the more ignoble part.

And maybe, as the higher light breaks in
  And shows the meaner task he has to do,
He is the greater that he strives to win
  Only the praise of being just and true.

For who can do no thing of sovran worth
  Which men shall praise, a higher task may find,
Plodding his dull round on the common earth,
  But conquering envies rising in the mind.

And God works in the little as the great
  A perfect work, and glorious over all—
Or in the stars that choir with joy elate,
  Or in the lichen spreading on the wall.

Constraint.

I would not that another eye should see
  What I now write, or other ear should hear.
  Then wherefore do I write it, being clear
To me, unwrit? and O the pain to me!
I hide my heart, and yet unbare it here,
  Then hide what I have writ, and mean to burn;
  I gather life's grey ashes in an urn,
And brood o'er them with many a dropping tear,
Dreading to keep, yet shrinking to destroy
  The treasured relics. O my Love! my bliss!
Is it all ashes now, that infinite joy?
  Leaving no other joy to me but this,
That I must open the old wound, and take
This blood from it, or else my heart will break.

The House in the Square.

The House in the Square.

O the House in the Square! dear House in the
 . Square !
 With the little grass-plots, and the mouldy green
 tubs
 Where the hoops fell away from the pale-flowering
 shrubs ;
But the widow was kind, and her daughters were fair,
And all the day long there was sunshine there,
 In the House in the Square.

A poor scholar's widow who still had her share
 Of life's vexing troubles, how kindly she took
 To our thoughtful life busy with lecture and book !
And with motherly heart she would sweeten our care
O'er the mild cup of tea, and the homely fare
 Of the House in the Square.

To her all the way of our life we laid bare,
 Its hopes and its fears, and she made them her
   own,
 And soothed us, or cheered us, as one who had
   known
The outlets that open in depths of despair;
And we all came away with a lightsomer air
  From the House in the Square.

The widow was kind; but her daughters were rare,
 Bright girls—our Muriel, Myra, and Loo:
 Nimble their fingers, their wits nimble too,
And like sunbeams and singing of birds, unaware
Of the brightness they brought, they would trip up
   the stair
  Of the House in the Square.

Never maidens more frank, never maidens more
   fair,
 Never maidens were simpler or truer than they;
 They could think as we thought, yet their hearts
   were as gay
As the feather-head fribbles that simper and stare,
When you speak as we spoke all the long evenings
   there
  .At the House in the Square.

There our Logic we aired, splitting many a hair;
  And the quick-witted girls, skilled in mellow-toned
      Greek,
  Reading just what we read, of their Plato would
      speak,
Or they sang an old song, or they played a blithe air,
When discussion grew hot about any affair
    In the House in the Square.

Their father, a scholar, would have them beware
  How they squandered their lives on the shallow
      and sweet;
  They should know what men knew, to be helps
      to them meet;
And the learning he loved he was eager to share
With the daughters he loved, until death found him
      there
    At the House in the Square.

We were all of us poor; but we did not much care,
  For we sought the best riches of wisdom and truth
  With the courage of faith, and the ardour of youth;
And with Homer and Shakespeare for friends, we
      could bear
The dust of the carriage that passed with a stare
    At the House in the Square.

How it haunts me, that home with its scholarly air!
  Those brave, gentle souls 'mid the city's turmoil,
  All so earnest in thought, and so patient in toil,
And so true to the right, and so patient to bear!
Ah! would I were now as I wont to be there
  At the House in the Square!

Muriel.

Whoever looked at Muriel, said :
  That girl has soul, her heart is high.
And she has great thoughts in her head,
  And scorn of meanness in her eye ;
How sweetly gracious she can smile !
Yet she looks haughty all the while,
And beams on you in the goddess style.

Whoever spoke to Muriel, thought :
  Her looks are nothing to her speech ;
That girl a noble strain has got,
  And soars beyond the common reach ;
Yet with her high and daring mood,
And with her faith in human good,
Will she be ever understood ?

Was it Mary Stuart, or Joan of Arc,
  Or Charlotte Corday that lived in her?

Did she bewitch with glances dark,
  Or make your noblest pulses stir?
Shall he who seeks her love to win,
Ere he gather its harvest in,
Be great in spirit, or great in sin?

A fair enigma! Low-browed, small,
  Yet walking in her queenly grace,
You would have vowed her stately, tall,
  Like Dian coming from the chase,
With bow unstrung, and flushed with pride,
The quivered arrows by her side,
Every tip with crimson dyed.

Was she a flirt whose roving eyes
  Entangled hearts with cunning wiles?
Or was she maiden without disguise,
  Bright with sunny and artless smiles?
What was the subtle charm that wrought,
So that, hopeful or hoping nought,
Still to win her love men sought?

And when she spoke in homeliest strain,
  What was the spell that held them fast?
And when she smote their hearts with pain,
  What was the glamour o'er them cast,

That she had but to smile anew,
And close to her again they drew,
Holding her all that is good and true?

Still in extremes of good or ill,
  She seemed to play a fateful part;
Some felt it bliss to do her will,
  Some found in it an aching heart;
But let them joy or let them ache,
The task she set them they would make
Their chiefest business for her sake.

She did not wonder at her lot,
  But, all unconscious, held her way,
Nor cared for incense that she got,
  Nor heeded what the world might say:
Unwittingly her spells she wove,
And sweetly lived apart, above
All the surmise of hate or love.

A beautiful enigma she,
  Our Muriel, with the dark bright eyes!
And still her beauty seemed to be
  Flashed on you with a fresh surprise:
And when they left her, men would look
As if inspired by some great Book
That did their meaner soul rebuke.

C

Loo.

Loo, Loo ! rather handsome than pretty,
Deft at a pudding, or stocking, or ditty,
    Quick at a riddle, and keen in retort ;
Knitting her brows now o'er polyglot learning,
Then toiling hard at her sewing and darning,
    Brimful of life, or at work or in sport.

Loo, Loo ! where on earth can she be ?
A Frau they tell me in Germany,
    Seeing to Saur Kraut, plump and fair :
Now in the store-room, now at the dresser,
Kitchen-maid, waiting-maid to her Professor,
    Just as she was at the House in the Square.

Loo, Loo ! she will toil at his Greek,
Help his prelections, and fittingly speak
    To scholars of Homer, to Burschen of beer,
Will search out in Plato the reference-passage,

And see to the Calf's-flesh, the cabbage and sausage,
And the pipe and the mug and the old household
gear.

Loo, Loo! she can sew, she can spin,
Can boil, stew and fry, see to flagon and binn,
Read the "Birds" and the "Clouds" with fine
sense of the fun,
Grasp Aeschylus' thought of the Fates, and the
Human
That softly gleams out in Euripides' Woman,
Then seek the Beer-garden, and knit in the sun.

Loo, Loo! what will she not do
For a husband she loves, ever faithful and true?
Is he off to the Sanskrit? she'll study the Veds:
And Babylon's stone-books and arrow-head letters,
O, she'll find the trick of them as soon as her betters,
And then turn to making shirt-collars or beds.

Loo, Loo! it was always her way;
She said men were failures, and had had their day,
But women were versatile, nimble as air,
Fit for the humblest tasks, fit for the highest,
Pouring life-blood into themes that were driest.—
Happy Professor, put under her care!

Myra.

She was the fairest of all the three;
   Yet not at first she caught the eye,
For in her maiden meekness she
   Wooed shadow like the primrose shy,
And seventeen summers hardly brought
   Her lissome form to perfect grace,
And the great purple eyes still shot
   Too large a light on the oval face;
Yet she was fairest of all the three,
E'en were she nothing at all to me.

She was the wisest of them, though
   Not so nimble and deft of wit;
But her heart thought, and made her know
   What for the loving heart was fit;
And when you touched on higher chords,
   With eager eyes and parted lips
You caught her listening to your words,
   Quick with mind to the finger-tips:

For she was wisest of all the three,
Had she been nothing at all to me.

She was the sweetest of them—sweet
　　As summer air from clover field;
And had a charity complete,
　　A touch, too, and a word that healed,
And therewith O so blithe a heart !
　　That she would laugh as birds must sing,
But could not play a bitter part
　　That she might say a clever thing.
Wisest, sweetest, fairest she,
E'en were she nothing at all to me.

And she was all the world to me;
　　I loved her though she knew it not,
And she loved, though I did not see
　　She gave me back the love I sought;
We loved, and yet we never wist
　　Till many years had come and gone,
We never spoke it, never kissed,
　　But loved in silence and alone.
Fairest, dearest of all the three,
O she was all the world to me.

Love.

O what is this that in my heart is singing,
  Like sweet bird, caged there, carolling all day?
O what is this such gladness to me bringing
  That life is bliss, and work is merry play,
And round my steps lo ! sunny flowers are springing
  As I go singing, singing on my way?
      O Love, glad Love !

Ah ! what is this that in my heart is sighing,
  Like captive vainly moaning to be free?
Ah ! what is this so heavy in me lying,
  No rest there is, nor any work for me,
And leaf and flower are drooping now and dying
  As I go sighing, sighing wearily?
      O Love, sad Love !

What thing is this my foolish heart is dreaming,
  That I should love, and long for yon bright star?

I sigh or sing, but she, unmoved, is gleaming
  As in high glory where the angels are—
I but a glow-worm on the earth dull-beaming,
  While she is gleaming, gleaming there afar.
    O Love, vain Love!

Speechless.

O thou fire-edged cloudlet
 Brimming o'er with light !
Like my heart thou hangest
 'Twixt the day and night.

Silently thou hangest,
 Seemingly at rest,
Yet there is strange tumult
 Boiling in thy breast.

O my heart o'er-brimming
 With burning thought of her,
Could'st thou only speak it,
 How her heart must stir !

But my love is surging,
 Like the hurrying wave
Breaking on the silence
 Of the dripping cave ;

Breaking on the silence
  Of the tangled shelf,
And falling back in foam-bells
  Still upon itself.

The Licentiate.

Dill's Lodgings.

I see the little dingy street,
   The little room three stories high,
The little woman, clean and neat,
   With kindly smile, and kindling eye,
The paper chintz, the staring prints,
   The bird whose carol would not cease,
And the cracked china ornaments
   Ranged stiffly on the mantel-piece.

A dingy street among the poor,
   Thronging with children day and night,
With sluttish women at every door
   Gossipping in the waning light:
Yet O the nights I there have seen!
   The humour kindling every face,
The play of wit, the logic keen
   That glorified the homely place!

Simple our life, with little change,
  And yet it was a bright romance,
Fresh with the wonderful and strange
  Of youth's enchanted golden trance;
How fresh in powers, in faiths, in thoughts!
  How full that fertile time appears!
We jotted down in pregnant notes
  The sum of all the after years.

The scholar's aim we held aloft,
  The fearless search for what is true,
As fresh discoveries called us oft
  Old schemes of Nature to review,
And to adjust the thought and fact,
  And to make room for growth yet more,
And to believe that God may act
  In ways we had not dreamed before.

We had our passing hours of doubt,
  But did not nurse the shadowy throng,
For we had work to go about
  That would not hold with doubting long.
And looking back on those brave years,
  Unspotted by the world and free,
Meagre and poor to-day appears,
  When earth is so much more to me.

Confidence.

Strange, that for all the wrecks upon the shore,
   And all that, helpless, drift about the sea,
   We never dream that such our fate may be,
Or shrink from life that may be one wreck more!

But fresh hope comes to each fresh soul, as light
   Dawns on the waters, dimpling in their waves,
   With running laughter tripping o'er the graves
Where former hopes lie buried out of sight.

And we are sure, and eager for the race,
   And crowd all sail, and deem not for an hour
   That life is not worth living, or that power
Is not in us to master time and space.

Is it that Nature, with a wanton's smile,
   Allures, but to delude, and break our hearts,
   Or worse than break them, when the soul departs
Of nobleness, that dwelt in us erewhile?

Or does she seem to us what we desire,
  Though herself true, and hating all deceit,
  And all we hear is but our own heart's beat,
And all we see but what our dreams inspire?

Scattered.

Scattered to East and West and North,
　　Some with the faint heart, some the stout,
Each to the battle of life went forth,
　　And all alone we must fight it out.

We had been gathered from cot and grange,
　　From the moorland farm, and the terraced street,
Brought together by chances strange,
　　And knit together by friendships sweet.

Not in the sunshine, not in the rain,
　　Not in the night of the stars untold,
Shall we ever all meet again,
　　Or be as we were in the days of old.

But as ships cross, and more cheerily go
　　Having changed tidings upon the sea.
So I am richer by them, I know,
　　And they are not poorer, I trust, by me.

D

Waiting.

Wearily drag the lagging hours
 To him who, waiting to be hired,
 Is by enforcëd idlesse tired
More than by strain of all his powers :
 Wearily, having in his heart
 The hope to play a worthy part,
 And scorning each ignoble art.

Girt for the fight, he waits forlorn,
 And O ! it irks him sore to rest,
 And watch, too oft with mocking jest,
Things done that fill his soul with scorn,
 As he with folded hands must sit,
 While lesser men, with scanty wit,
 Get all the work, and tangle it.

So life grows bitter ; or perhaps
 Hope flirts a moment in his face,
 Then trips off to another place,
And pours its treasures in the laps

Of some dull souls whose easy feet
Will tread the old familiar beat,
Contented getting much to eat.

And lo ! the work remains undone,
　And work is what he hungers for,
　But cannot find an open door,
And loiters idly in the sun,
　Still waiting with his heart on fire,
　And wasting with its great desire,
Waiting and finding none to hire.

A Wish.

Just a path that is sure,
    Thorny or not,
And a heart honest and pure,
Keeping the path that is sure,
    That be my lot:
Life is no merry-making,
Hark! how the waves are breaking!

Just plain duty to know,
    Irksome or not,
And truer and better to grow
In doing the duty I know,
    That I have sought:
Life is no merry-making,
How the stiff pine trees are quaking!

Just to keep battling on,
    Weary or not,

Sure of the Right alone,
As I keep battling on,
   For the true thought:
Life is no merry-making,
Ah! how men's hearts are breaking!

Self-Contempt.

I bear a message to the sons of men,
 Faithful and true,
And it should drop on earth like tender rain,
But yet I bear my message all in vain,
 For let me do
Whate'er I may, and plead howe'er I can,
 I touch no heart of man.

How should I? Though I bear a message true,
 The thing I want
Is, room for me to live, and work to do;
And so I go about to places new
 With patience scant,
And tell my tale, and then go on my way,
 And life grows dull and grey.

And I am full of self-contempt and scorn
 To go about

Thus falsely speaking truth to hearts forlorn,
And jibe myself that I, some ugly morn,
    Shall be found out
To be no prophet whom the Lord hath sent,
    Or for His service meant.

But is my message true? To-day, I seem
    Full of the lights
That from the bleeding Christ so grandly stream;
And lo! to-morrow, it is like a dream
    Of restless nights:
And I have drifted back into the shade,
    Unsaying what I said.

I seek a gospel which I should have found
    Before I tried
To preach, with unfixed heart, the faith profound
Which tells the captive that he is unbound
    By Him who died
To ope his prison door, and set him free
    From all his misery.

O heart that would be true! O hard estate,
    To falset bound!
This only comfort is there in my fate;
My message I did ne'er prevaricate
    With tinkling sound

To tickle ears, nor played with shewy trick
    Of tinsel Rhetoric.

I've mocked myself, and laughed with bitter jest
    At much I saw;
But yet I kept a true heart in my breast,
Nor turned in all my trouble and unrest
    From the high law
Of present duty; and my peace is great
    Even in this hard estate.

Hope.

A little Kirk, beneath a steep green hill,
  With a grey spire that peeps o'er tall elm-trees,
In a still, pastoral land of brook and rill,
And broomy knoll, and sleepy, dripping mill,
  Far from the stir of cities and of seas :

And near the Kirk, low nestling in the copse,
  With honeysuckle clad, and roses red,
A little Manse, whose sweet-flowered garden slopes
Down to the river where the river drops
  With murmuring ripple o'er a pebbly bed.

How happily the days and years might flow
  Among the silent shepherds brooding long,
In pious labour, studious to know,
And patient service, till their life should grow
  From thoughtful silence into thoughtful song;

To pass from house to house in visit free,
  Welcome as sunshine at the smoking hearth,

To take the little children on the knee,
And bless them, as He did in Galilee,
   Who came with blessing unto all the earth ;

To speak to them of Duty and of God,
   And of the Love that clasped the bitter Cross,
And of the health and comfort of His rod,
And go before them on the way He trod,
   Who found Life's glory and fulness in its loss ;

To share in all the joys and griefs they have,
   To bless the bridal, not else thought complete,
To stand beside the cradle and the grave,
And tell them how the meek and true and brave,
   Turn graves to cradles where the sleep is sweet.

O happy lot ! with one, to brighten life,
   Smiling soft-eyed beside the evening fire,
Sharing the sorrow, sweetening all the strife,
And leaning on her lord, a loving wife,
   And cherished by her lord with fond desire.

Dream of the golden gloaming of the day !
   Dream of the night beneath the folding star !
Dream of the hungry heart that in me lay !
Dream by the river rippling soft away
   Into the tremulous moonshine—which dreams are.

The Brook and the River.

A stream from the heath-purpled mountain
    Comes, with a gush,
From the star-moss round its fountain,
    Breaking the hush
Of the silent, songless mountain.

Peewit-and-curlew-haunted,
    Foaming, it flows
There where the wild deer undaunted
    Bells, as it goes
Peewit-and-curlew-haunted.

It plays with the rowan and bracken,
    And grey lichened stone,
But never its pace will it slacken,
    Still hurrying on,
Though it plays with the rowan and bracken.

A river winds 'neath the shadows
    Of pine-wood and oak,

And hums to the bee-humming meadows,
  And the white flock
That bleats from the mists and the shadows.

Down to the still river hastens
  The swift-flowing stream,
And aye as the distance it lessens
  Its bright waters gleam,
And it leaps and sparkles and hastens,

Till in the calm-flowing river
  Softly it sinks,
And hears not and heeds not for ever
  What fern or tree thinks,
But only the low-whispering river.

O Love ! my river full-flowing,
  Wait, wait for me ;
O Love ! my love, ever-growing,
  Hastens to thee
For rest in thy river calm-flowing.

Failure.

I see the Kirk beneath the hill,
  The tall elms rustling in the breeze,
The modest Manse, so calm and still,
The dripping of the sleepy mill
  That hides among the nutting trees.

I look down, with a hungry heart,
  On the broad river rippling cool;
The fisher plies his patient art,
The trout leaps, and the May flies dart
  About the slowly eddying pool.

Low sunbeams on the meadows play,
  The moon shews like a film of cloud,
A star from the red skirts of day
Peeps to another star far away,
  And the hill is wrapt in a misty shroud.

A shepherd's wife comes to the door,
   Shading her eyes with large brown hand,
He is away on the upland moor,
And nothing she sees but a kestrel soar,
   Keen-eyed, spying over the land.

There is no voice but the rushing rills,
   And creak of frightened peewit's wing,
And bleat of young lambs on the hills,
Heard only when a silence fills
   The soul, and all the space of things.

What made my eyes grow dim and blind?—
   Ah, when the heart is heavy and low,
The beauty that on earth we find,
Or strain of music on the wind,
   Shall touch it like an utter woe!

Submission.

I will remember it for aye,
  Though there I was forgotten soon;
It haunts me in the sunny day,
  And under stars and moon.
It was the only hope I had
  That unto near fulfilment grew;
A while it made me very glad;
A while it made me very sad;
  And then I knew
'Twas but another thread He wove
In the mixed web of Father-love.

Moralizing.

Roses fair on thorns do grow;
And they tell me even so
Sorrows into virtues grow:
    Heigh-ho!
It was a stroke
Brought the stream from the flinty rock.

Frosty winter kills out weeds;
And they tell me evil seeds
Die out in the heart that bleeds:
    Heigh-ho!
And some have faith
That dying is the death of Death.

Ah! the loss may yet be gain,
Bitter bliss may spring from pain,
As the bird-songs after rain:
    Heigh-ho!
But nought shall be
Ever again the same to me.

Crystallized Sermon.

E

Note.

He had no written sermons, only took
Brief jottings upon any scrap of paper—
Bits of old letters, envelopes, or labels—
And there the thought was scrawled, but half the
      matter
Was illustration roughly etched, a kind
Of hieroglyph whereof he had the key,
Now lost for ever: etchings strongly drawn,
With a clear eye for form, and touched with humour
Or pathos; so he penned his similes.
But certain thoughts that took his fancy more,
And, as I guess, had troubled hearers more,
These he had gathered up, and put in verse,
As sermon-matter crystallized, once spoken
In amplitude of phrase, but now compact;
Not to be preached, but crooned in quiet hours
Of musing by the fire. Poor sermons truly

For common folk with common thoughts and sins
And sorrows, and no reaching out of hope
To find a larger faith in Charity;
Yet notable for a Licentiate
Starting, on Saturdays, with little valise
And threadbare garments, for some homely kirk
Among the hills, or on the village green,
Whither he went, and fired his aimless shot,
Then passed away again, and was forgot.

Sacrifice.

"And there he builded an altar unto the Lord that appeared
unto him."—Gen. xii. 7.

Is there Bridge-maker who can throw
   An arch across the gulf of years,
That we may travel back, and know
   The brooding thoughts, and haunting fears,
And clinging faiths of them who raised
   Their altars 'neath the evening star,
And offered to the gods, and praised,
   And drave the dogs and birds afar?

Vainly, I seek to know his mind
   Who smote the lamb with gleaming knife,
And sprinkled blood, and hoped to find
   The peace of a diviner life.
Far off he seems, I cannot tell
   Whether beneath me, or above,
Or compassed round with shades of hell,
   Or trembling in the bliss of love!

I gaze back from this brink of time
　　On shadowy forms of early days,
That, in the morning, loom sublime,
　　God-guided on untravelled ways;
But o'er the vague, vast chasm that parts
　　Their thought from mine I cannot go;
I wot not how their troubled hearts
　　Were calmed by making blood to flow.

Yet once wherever man had trod,
　　Or sin had grown from base desire,
He built an altar to his god,
　　And laid the faggot on the fire,
And brought the choicest of the flock
　　From frolic by its bleating dam,
And laid upon the unhewn rock
　　The tender kid, or spotless lamb.

The knife into its throat was driven,
　　The blood was sprinkled on the stone,
The smell of fat went up to heaven,
　　That on the leaping flame was thrown;
And he before his god was glad,
　　And prayed, and sang his evening hymn,
And laid him down to sleep, and had
　　Bright dreams until the stars grew dim.

Thus did the Hebrew on the plain
  Of Moreh, while Heaven, many-eyed,
Unweeping, saw the throbbing pain,
  Or smiled even as the victim died,
And smelled a sweeter smell from blood,
  He wist, than from the myriad flowers
That breathed, from shining bell and bud,
  Their incense through the dewy hours.

The subtle-witted Greek with art
  Was fain the anguish to adorn,
And singing with a sprightly heart,
  Led the young kid with sprouting horn,
Flower-garlanded, into the grove,
  And there by crystal fount or brook,
Into the life of Nature wove
  The slender thread of life he took.

The Norseman slew the mighty steed
  That bore him in the battle fray,
And ate the flesh, and drank the mead,
  And feasted Hella-thoughts away,
And piled the logs upon the hearth,
  And called the gods, in stormy words,
To send the hungry ravens forth
  To fatten at the feast of swords.

Yet darker rites were theirs who kissed
  Their hand unto the placid moon ;
Or who the Tyrian Moloch wist
  To pacify with choicest boon
Of babe or maid ; or where the Priest
  Stood grim beneath the Druid oak :
Or Aztec fed with ample feast
  The captives for the fateful rock.

What was it entered thus the soul,
  To give it calm, or promise bliss ?
Strange that the ages, as they roll,
  Have dropped behind a thought like this,
Which held the universal mind
  Of all the world when it was young !
For now the key I cannot find
  In all that men have said or sung.

In mocking scorn, the Prophet laughed
  Loud at a hungering, thirsting God
Who craved the flesh of bulls, or quaffed
  The reeking blood that dyed the sod,
For every beast is His, and all
  The cattle with their clover-breath,
And Love that quickened great and small
  Can feel no pleasure in their death.

They say the Giver of all life
  Is fain to take the life He gives,
And will not spare, unless the knife
  May gash some other thing that lives;
And they are sure, and they are clear,
  While I in dizzying darkness grope,
But trust that God will yet appear
  In star-gleams of a nobler hope.

I would not heed, though that old Faith
  'Had spread its roots o'er all the earth,
If they were withered now in death
  As having no abiding worth :
But from those roots still branches spring
  That shape our thoughts of truth and right,
And still of Sacrifice we sing,
  And blood that maketh clean and white.

There was some passion, fear, or guilt
  That emphasized expression thus,
As by a mighty oath, and felt
  A peace it cannot give to us.
But what ? Was it the soul's consent
  To die for sin that it had done ?
Nay ; man's strong life was not yet spent
  On threads by morbid conscience spun.

I know the anguish that is wrought
    Into the web of highest bliss ;
I know the Cross must be his lot
    Who thrills with Love's redeeming kiss.
But when the Lamb or Bullock fell
    'Neath the keen blade, or shattering blow,
How that could make the sick heart well,
    Or nearer God—I do not know.

And yet the Lamb of God was slain
    Or ere the age of sin began,
And wrapt in that prophetic pain
    Is all the history of man ;
And all the fulness of his life,
    And all the greatness of his thought,
And all the peace of his long strife
    Root in that Everlasting Ought.

The Standing Stones.

"God at sundry times and in divers manners spake in time past
unto the fathers."—Heb. i. 1.

A rolling upland, open and bare,
  A blasted heath where the night wind moans,
Eerie and weird, to the curlews there,
And the greedy kite and the kestrel scare
Singing birds from the lightsome air.

High on the heath are the Standing Stones,
  Great, gaunt stones in a mystic ring,
Girdling a barrow where heroes' bones
Crumble to dust of death that owns
Them and their wars and faiths and thrones.

Not far off is an oozy spring
  Feeding a black and dismal pool;
There slow efts crawl, horse-leeches cling,
And the dragon-fly whirrs on restless wing,
And near by the adder is coiled in the ling;

And once an oak made a shadow cool,
  Woven of its green boughs overhead,
And blithe birds sang in the leafage full;
Now but a raven, bird of dule,
Croaks on its stump from May to Yule.

But silently watching the silent dead
  Stands the grey circle of sentinels,
Scarred and lichened, as ages sped
With snows, and dripping rains overhead,
And suns, and the wasteful life they bred.

Now, evermore where the dead man dwells
  The living have gone to seek for God,
And the Altar-fire of the Unseen tells,
Or the swing and the clash of Christian bells
Summon to Lauds and Canticles.

And there, of old, in that bleak abode
  Of wily lapwing and shrill curlew,
To circle and cairn they carried their load
Of burdened thought, as they wearily trod
On to the brink where they lost the road.

There dipped the Sun in the dripping dew
  His earliest beams; and there he met

The Bel-fire kindling its answer true—
Light for the light in heaven that grew,
Worship-light to the Light-god due.

So men acknowledged, and paid their debt,
  In the old days, to the powers above,
Giving back that they were fain to get,
And piling the faggots, dry or wet,
Still as the keen stars rose and set.

Was not the instinct true that wove
  Fire-worship thus for the god of fire ?
Give from below what ye get from above,
Light for the heaven-light, Love for its Love,.
A holy soul for the Holy Dove.

God tunes for Himself the hallowed lyre
  That shall truly His praises shew;
He gives the song that He will desire,
Ever new from the trembling wire,
Ever new from the heart on fire.

Back to its fountain let it flow
  Whatsoever He sends to you ;
Mercy, if mercy of His ye know,
And if your joy He has made to grow,
Up to Him let its gladness go.

So in all faiths there is something true,
    Even when bowing to stock or stone—
Something that keeps the Unseen in view
Beyond the stars, and beyond the blue,
And notes His gifts with the worship due.

For where the spirit of man has gone
    A-groping after the Spirit divine,
Somewhere or other it touches the Throne,
And sees a light that is seen by none,
But who seek Him that is sitting thereon.

Seek but provision of bread and wine,
    High-ceiled houses, and heaps of gold,
Fools to flatter, and raiment fine,
All the wealth of the sea and mine—
And nothing of God shall e'er be thine.

But who seeks Him, in the dark and cold,
    With heart that elsewhere finds no rest,
Some fringe of the skirts of God shall hold,
Though round his spirit the mists may fold,
With eerie shadows, and fears untold.

The Ancient Cross.

"God at sundry times and in divers manners spake in time past
unto the fathers."—Heb. i. 1.

There is a long, green spit of land
    That juts into a loch; the sea
Not far off thuds upon the sand,
    Or crashes where the red rocks be;
But here the peace is very great,
    Small brooklets murmur as they list,
    And, green with oft-enfolding mist,
The hills stand round in quiet state.

The lady-birch, with drooping bough,
    Shews graceful by the sturdy pine;
And his red scales more ruddy glow
    The more her silver branches shine;
And here and there the rough-kneed oak
    Spreads its sharp-dinted glossy leaves
    Where the slow fisher, oaring, cleaves
Its shadow with a lazy stroke.

And on the spit of land a stone,
  With lichen tinted and with moss,
Stands on the tufted grass alone,
  Its face graven with a simple Cross,
There is no word of pious lore,
  Nor wreath, nor ring, nor ornament,
  Nor sacred letters nicely blent—
A simple Cross, and nothing more.

Not other is the stone from those
  That in the mystic circle stand;
An unhewn slab, and yet it shews
  New light risen on a darkling land;
In monumental speech, it tells
  The story of the ages gone,
  The story of a Pagan stone
New-charmed with sacred Christian spells.

Men had been giving blow for blow,
  And wrath for wrath, and tears for tears,
And reaping duly grief and woe
  Through the long tale of blood-stained years:
Still, with the summer, long ships steered
  Up the calm loch with Norsemen fierce,
  Whose gleaming swords were sharp to pierce,
And neither gods nor men they feared.

In vain the coracle was hid
  In cove beneath the branching trees ;
In vain they practised rites forbid,
  Or sought the hills, and shunned the seas ;
The Viking came with brass-beaked ship,
  And wrath and sorrow came with him,
  And many a shining eye grew dim,
And quivered many a smiling lip.

Lo ! then there travelled o'er the sea,
  From the lone isle where saints were bred,
A peaceful, unarmed company
  Who brought good news of God, they said :
They suffered much, yet did not grieve,
  They laboured much, and wearied not,
  They bore with joy a bitter lot,
And sang their hymns at morn and eve.

They sang about the dim grey seas,
  And One that walked upon their wave ;
They sang about the streams and trees
  In a far land beyond the grave ;
And when Norse axe, or wild kerne's knife,
  Unpitying, smote bare head or breast,
  They sweetly sang themselves to rest
With songs about the Crown of Life.

F

By suffering thus subduing wrath,
   They conquered those who vanquished them;
And corn grew on the waste war-path,
   And nets dried where the long ships came,
And there was wealth where had been loss,
   And ringing bells for clash of swords,
   And needing no explaining words,
On the old stone they graved a Cross.

They conquered; yet for many a day
   The fierce old spirit lingered still,
And the hot passion had its sway,
   And the old war-gods wrought their will,
And rites of fear and blood were done
   Amid the mists, and on the moss;
   They had but scratched a shallow Cross
Upon the grim old Pagan stone.

Ah me! and still we hardly know
   The depth and glory of the Faith
That opens life to man by slow,
   Meek suffering, patient unto death;
We still are fain, with wrath and strife,
   To seek for gain, to shrink from loss,
   Content to scratch our shallow Cross
On the rough surface of old life.

And there it stands, the cross-charmed stone,
  On the green spit beyond the trees ;
It hears by night the faint sea-moan,
  By day the song-bird and the breeze,
And Christian bells, and sounding trains,
  And the hard grinding of the wheels ;
  And now and then a pilgrim kneels,
And tells to it his griefs and pains.

The Abbey.

"God at sundry times and in divers manners spake in time past
unto the fathers."—Heb. i. 1.

Near by the river the Abbey stands,
Among old fruit trees, and on fat green lands,
   With a weir on the river to drive the mill.
And cunning cruives at the salmon-leap;
And the beeves on the clover are fetlock-deep,
   And the sheep are nibbling the grassy hill.

'Tis now but a ruin spreading wide
Broken gable and cloistered side
   'Mong lichened pear-trees and Spanish nuts,
Here a pillar, and there a shrine,
Or niche where its sculptured lords recline:—
   Long a quarry for walls and huts.

O stately the Lady-Chapel there
Once reared its cross in the upper air
   Near by the river among the trees,

And sweet bells rung, and censers swung,
And matins and vespers and lauds were sung
  With solemn-chaunted litanies.

O'er the high Altar a meek face shone,
A virgin-mother and baby-son,
  Fashioned by art beyond the sea;
And there, in linen or purple dressed,
A priest gave thanks, or a priest confessed,
  With a psalm of praise, or a bended knee.

And some would pore over vellum books,
And some would feather the sharp fish-hooks,
  And some would see to the sheep and kine;
Some went hunting the red-deer stag,
Some would travel with beggar's bag,
  And some sat long by the old red wine;

Some would go pleading a cause in Rome,
And still found cause to be far from home,
  And near to St. Peter's costly door:
They were not all bad, and they were not all good
Who wore the Monk's girdle and sandal and hood,
  But some of them padded the Cross they bore.

Yet was the Abbey a fruitful stage
In the slow growth, and the ripening age
  Of the long history of man:

For beaming virgin, and holy child
Made many a fierce heart meek and mild,
  And the mastery there of mind began.

The footsore pilgrim there found rest,
The heartsore too was a welcome guest,
  And who loved books, got helpful store.
It is God who guides the world's affairs,
And ever it rises by winding stairs,
  Screwing its way from the less to more.

He reads the story best, who reads
Ever to find some germing seeds
  Sprouting up to a nobler end,
And God's long patience working still
Through all the good, and through all the ill,
  And always something in us to mend.

From bud to bell the wild bee strays,
Seeking the sweets of the sunny days,
  Probing deep for the honey-cell;
Yet well for his theft he pays the flower,
For he brings to the blossom a quickening power,
  And a richer life to bud and bell.

Narrow and poor was the old Church-life
As it prayed in its cell, amid storm and strife,
  With scourgings many, and fastings new;

It knew no letters, it spurned at Art,
It had no pleasures, and lived apart—
  Doomed to die as the world's life grew.

But something of wisdom the Monk would know,
Something of gladness here below,
  Something of beauty, and what it can;
He was not sinless, and yet he brought
A larger heart, and a freer thought,
  And a fuller life to the sons of man.

And we are a stage too—not the end;
Others will come yet our work to mend,
  And they too will wonder at our poor ways.
Ah! Life is more than our sermons, prayers,
Bourses, machineries, multiplied wares—
  Still the heart sighs for the better days.

Still is a feeling of something in me
Which yet I am not, and I ought to be,
  Vaguely reaching for more and more;
And the gain is loss, when I do not win
Larger life for the soul within,
  And hopes of an ever-opening door.

A Parabolic Discourse.

"A certain man planted a vineyard, and let it forth to husbandmen,
and went into a far country."—Luke xx. 9.

First Head of Discourse.

A stately mansion in its park
　　Stands fair amid the oaks and limes,
Throstle and ousel, cuckoo and lark,
　　And flowers and shrubs of many climes,
　　And stars and tides ring out the chimes,
　　Telling the seasons and the times.

And many guests there come and go,
　　And make themselves at home in it,
Some restless, hurrying to and fro,
　　Some lounging where the sunbeams flit,
　　Some with a curious craving smit,
　　Some with the laugh of careless wit.

All through the woods they hunt the game,
  Or snare the fish in brook and mere,
They bake the wheat by the ruddy flame,
  Or roast the flesh of the fatted steer,
  And draw from cellars cool the clear
  Old wine that has ripened many a year.

This stately mansion is their inn,
  Where many fret, and all make free ;
They set the tables to lose or win,
  They tune the strings to dance with glee :
  Only their Host they do not see,
  And many doubt if Host there be.

They think He has been long away,
  And that the place is theirs by right;
They think, if He were coming, they
  Could bear the searching of His light;
  They think He is a dream of night,
  That morn will banish from the sight.

But there are some grave men and wise
  Who lead the guests to a silent room,
Wherein a golden volume lies,
  And picture of One in youthful bloom,
  Whose face a glory doth illume ;
  And by His side are a Cross and Tomb.

And this, they say, is He who made
  The great house 'mong the oaks and limes,
And He is living who once was dead,
  But far away in heavenly climes,
  Where are no stars or tides or chimes,
  Telling the seasons and the times.

And some of His guests He keeps for bliss,
  And some of them He keeps for gloom,
Some He seals with a loving kiss,
  And some He stamps with the brand of doom,
  Some He saves by Cross and Tomb,
  Meekly dying in their room.

These He loves of very grace ;
  Those He leaves to die in sin,
Nevermore to see His face,
  Never hope of life to win :
  All the unbelieving kin
  Wrath Eternal shuts them in.

And therefore all should bow the knee
  At the glory of His might,
Glory of His justice see,
  Surely doing all things right ;
  And in Him should they delight
  Whether He heal their hearts, or smite.

SECOND HEAD OF DISCOURSE.

Once, pitying much their foredoomed lot,
  One came who gentle was and meek,
And burdened with long-brooding thought,

And when he heard the wise men speak,
  He deeply questioned them; and they
Replied that he was vain and weak:

For this had been the faith alway
  Of all the martyrs and the saints,
And all the ages stretching grey

Among the mountains of events,
  Since Luther held the world at bay,
Or Paul was busy making tents.

Then silently he turned away,
  And to himself the question put,
Searching the matter, night and day.

He did not argue nor dispute,
  But prayed that God would lead him right,
And sat and brooded still and mute,

Until he saw, as 'twere, the white
  Thin sickle of the new-born moon
That yet holds all the round of light,

And all to him grew clear as noon,
  And he came singing like a bird
That sings for very joy its tune :

He deemed it the Eternal Word,
  The glory and the life of Heaven,
Which his entranced soul had heard.

Lo ! I have sought, he said, and striven
  To find the truth, and found it not,
But yet to me it hath been given,

And unto you it hath been brought.
  This Host of ours our Father is,
And we the children He begot.

Upon my brow I felt His kiss,
  His love is all about our steps,
And He would lead us all to bliss ;

For though He comes in many shapes,
  His love is throbbing in them all,

And from His love no soul escapes,
And from His mercy none can fall.

Third Head of Discourse.

Now, when they heard his words, they rose,
  And drove him forth into the night
With many bitter words like blows ;
  And said that all would now be right,
That all their trouble now would cease,
And all the house be full of peace.

Yet in the dark and in the cold,
  Out in the night among the dews,
He ceased not his discourse to hold
  Amid the limes and elms and yews ;
It was "a still small voice," and yet
They heard it in the wind and wet.

He wandered there among the trees,
  Or in the daylight, or the dark,
And in the whistling of the breeze
  They heard him singing like a lark ;
He is our Father dear, he cried,
And for the love of man He died.

And somehow ever as he sang
   It seemed as if the great Book shone,
And mystic, pleading voices rang
   About the rooms of vaulted stone,
And tears were on the pictured face,
And it was like a haunted place.

But they went on as they had done,
   Still eating of the earth's increase,
Laughing or lounging in the sun,
   And vowing that they had great peace ;
But no one heeded now the old
Strange story that the wise men told.

And yet the wise men were content,
   And said that they had faithful been ;
And to the chamber door they went,
   Though not by them the lights were seen,
And read the Book and sang and prayed,
And ate their viands undismayed.

FOURTH HEAD OF DISCOURSE.

Ah ! which is truth ?   The sovereign Will
   That worketh out a purpose vast,
   Beyond our ken, to end at last
In severance of the good and ill ?

Or love that sweetly would enfold
 All creatures in a large embrace,
 And with the tears that blot its face
Blot also out their sins untold?

Dear story of the Cross and Book !
 Is it our fabling hearts that speak
 Fond dreams in Thee ? and shall we seek,
In vain, through every field and nook

Of Nature for a witness true,
 Affirming what thy words have said
 Of Him who liveth, and was dead,
And liveth to make all things new?

In vain, we try to reconcile
 His hapless lot with love divine,
 Who born with taint of lust or wine
Is brought up in the lap of guile,

And gets no chance : his infant eyes
 Look out on riot, vice, and hate,
 And lies and blood, and horrors great,
And learn to look without surprise.

And yet I hold with them who say
 That God is love, and God is light ;

But this is faith, it is not sight,
And waiteth, hoping for the day.

'Tis vain to wrestle with the doubt,
  Or think to reason it away,
  As well go wrestle with the grey
Cold mist that creeps the hills about.

Yet I can trust, and I can praise,
  Weary and dark as is the road,
  Because I see the heart of God,
When on the bitter Cross I gaze.

O fellest deed of wrath and wrong !
  Yet in thine evil-seeming slept
  A large assurance that hath kept
The Faith of goodness calm and strong.

Elijah.

2 Kings ii. 2-11.

It was the great Elijah in the chariot of heaven,
With the horses of Jehovah, by a mighty angel
    driven,
And the chariot wheels were rushing 'mid a mist
    of fiery spray,
Through glory of the night to higher glory of the
    day.

It was the great Elijah—but meek and still was
    he,
For he trembled at the glory which his flesh was
    soon to see,
Going, girdled in his sackcloth, as the prophets
    were arrayed,
To the splendour of the Presence where the angels
    are dismayed.

Unwonted was the honour which his Master would
　　accord
To his true and faithful witness, bravest servant of
　　the Lord ;
But better had he borne, I trow, the sad old
　　human way
Of entering by the gates of Death into eternal
　　day.

Aye, better had he borne to turn his face unto
　　the wall,
With his kindred in their kindness gathered round
　　him, one and all,
And to lie down with his fathers in the dust for
　　some brief space ;
For the death, he once had dreaded, now appeared
　　a tender grace.

It was the great Elijah ; and the form that would
　　dilate
In the presence of King Ahab, and his Councillors
　　of State,
Now bowed its head in lowliness, as if it dared not
　　cope
With the terror of the glory, and the wonder of the
　　hope.

Away from earth they travelled ; yet he somehow
    seemed to know
The road, as if his weary steps had trod it long
    ago :
And was not that the wilderness to which he once
    had fled ?
And that the lonely juniper where he had wished
    him dead ?

And was not that the cave where he had sat in
    sullen mood,
Until he heard the "still small voice" that touched
    his heart with good ?
And was not that the road by which from Carmel
    he had run
Before the chariot of the king about the set of
    sun ?

Yea, God was backward leading him to heaven along
    the path
Which he had erewhile travelled o'er in fear or grief
    or wrath,
That by its mingled memories his heart He might
    prepare
For the grandeur and the glory and the crown he
    was to wear.

Now, as they drove, careering, with the fire-flakes
    round the wheels,
And the sparks that rushed like shooting stars from
    the horses' flashing heels,
Lo ! he was aware of a throng of men lay strewn
    along the road ;
And straight at them the angel drave the chariot of
    God.

"Stay, stay !" then cried Elijah, "rein up the fiery
    steeds ;
They will mangle those poor people lying there like
    bruised reeds ;
See, they stir not; they are sleeping; or their
    thoughts are far away,
And they do not hear the wheels of God to whom
    perchance they pray.

"Full oft have I been praying so, and chiding His
    delay,
And lo ! the work was done, or ere my lips had
    ceased to pray ;
For our ears are dull of hearing; stay, and put
    them not to proof
Beneath the grinding of the wheel, and trampling
    of the hoof."

" Nay, it boots not," said the angel, " they are but
the ghosts of those
Three hundred priests of Baalim who fell beneath
thy blows
That glorious day on Carmel; let them perish, as
they cry
To the gods that cannot help them when they live,
or when they die.

" Drive on, ye horses of the Lord, across the wel-
tering throng,
It is the great Elijah ye are bearing now along,
Let them see him once again in the triumph of his
faith,
And hear the bitter mockery, and taste the bitter
death."

It was the great Elijah, the prophet stern and
grand,
Faithful only to Jehovah he in all the faithless
land,
Zealous even unto slaughter for the God of
Israel
'Gainst Ahab and the minions of the Tyrian
Jezebel.

But he answered, " Stay thy running, and let me
      here descend,
For the Lord has brought me hither surely for this
      very end :
Ah ! this thing I had forgotten—day of glory and
      of dole—
And I wist not what did ail me, but its weight was
      on my soul."

Then he stept down from the chariot, looking O so
      meek and mild,
For the burden of the glory made him humble as
      a child ;
And he lifted up the prostrate head of one and
      then another,
For the burden of the greatness made him tender
      as a mother.

" Ye priests of ancient Sidon, and of purple Tyre,"
      he cried,
" I have heard a still small voice that hushed the
      storms of wrath and pride,
And God who was not in the fire, and was not in
      the wind,
Was in the still small voice that spake to the
      unquiet mind.

" O worshippers of Ashtaroth, and priests of Baalim,
I thought to please Jehovah, and I only grievëd
    Him ;
I flouted you, and mocked you, and I deemed that
    I did well
When I smote you in the name of Him, the God
    of Israel.

" But He hath no pleasure in the death of any man
    that dies,
He delighteth not in blood or smoke of such a
    sacrifice ;
Yea, not a worm is crushed, but the writhings of its
    pain
Touch a chord of His great pity who made nothing
    live in vain.

" He had patience with thee, Sidon, and patience I
    had none ;
For the art of Tyre, perchance, He let the sin of
    Tyre alone,
Something He saw to stay His wrath ; but I would
    nothing see ;
Ye were the Priests of Jezebel, and hateful unto
    me.

" I did not think how hard it is to find the way of
    truth ;
I did not think how hard it is to shake the faith
    of youth ;
Yet, if I was walking in the light, the credit was
    not mine,
But God's who in His grace to me had made the
    light to shine.

" If ye were walking in the dark, and I was in the
    light,
I should have brought its help to you, and plied
    you with its might;
But I made my heart a flaming fire, my tongue a
    bitter rod,
And I did not hear the still small voice which is
    the voice of God.

" I said ye might have right to live in Tyre beside
    the sea,
But not in high Samaria, or fertile Galilee ;
And I smote you there on Carmel, as I thought,
    by His commands,
But I smote my own heart also when your blood
    was on my hands.

" For the strength departed from me as the pity in
    me died,
And in an unloved loneliness I nursed unhallowed
    pride ;
And I wist there was none faithful on the earth,
    but only I,
And sat beneath the juniper, and prayed that I
    might die.

" For Jezebel and Ahab did as they had done
    before,
And the idols were exalted, and idolaters were
    more,
And the land was nothing better for the blood that
    had been shed,
And I sat beneath the juniper, and wished that I
    were dead.

"'Then it was I heard the still small voice, and
    bowed me to the ground,
Humbled by the gracious burden of the mercy I
    had found,
But I may not enter into rest, or with the Lord
    abide,
Till ye humble with your pardon him that smote
    you in his pride."

Then, one by one, he bore them gently from the
    angel's way,
And, one by one, he laid them down, and kissed
    them where they lay;
And he never was so human as in his meekness
    then,
And he never was so godlike till he was like other
    men.

And he said in yearning pity, "O that I might die
    for you,
Hapless souls that are in darkness, and who know
    not what they do!"
And the tearful eye was swimming, and he heaved
    a weary sigh;—
He was very near to glory with that great tear in
    his eye.

And the angel in his chariot sat, and watched him
    toiling long,
And the angel's face shone radiant, and he broke
    into a song;
For the choicest songs of angels are the anthems
    that begin
With the sorrow of a contrite heart a-breaking for
    its sin.

And ever as the prophet wept, the angel sang more
    loud,
And his face was shining more, the more the
    prophet's head was bowed ;
Until the task was ended, and the flesh was crucified,
When lo ! they were at the gate of heaven, and the
    door was opened wide.

Lo ! they were at the gate of heaven, and there a
    mighty throng,
Ten thousand times ten thousand, raised their shout,
    and sang their song,
But the Lord remembered he was flesh, and down-
    cast for his sin,
And Enoch who had walked with God came forth
    to lead him in.

Litterateur.

Note.

So he forsook the priesthood just in time,
And only just in time; for there had been
Ominous whispers, here and there, about
Doctrine unsound, unsettling, dangerous,
In rural manses, and at cleric meetings;
In smithies too, and where the shuttle clicked,
Sharp wits discussed him, and the ploughman even
Ceased whistling in the furrow, brooding o'er
The thoughts that came to him, and drove his soul
From its old furrow into a fresh soil.

Unsettling and alarming! There was peace
While the tea-table gossipped, and the smith
Told his coarse stories to the laughing clowns,
(Heard also by the maids that bleached the linen
Upon the green hard by)—peace when the weaver
Talked treason with his thin and bloodless lips,
Starved into revolutionary dreams—

And peace while men grew brutal as the steer
They harnessed to their plough ! Then all went well;
There was no danger to alarm the church !
But thought disturbs the world, and thought of God
Unsettles most of all; for it is life,
And only life can comprehend its force,
Or guide it. 'Tis as lightning in the cloud;
We know not what, or where its bolt may strike,
But fear for the church-steeples, and ourselves,
Nor dream there may be blessing even in it.
Yet there are surely times when there is nought
So needed as unsettling, just to get
Out of old ruts, and seek a nobler life.
Raban forsook the church, whose service once
Had been his fond ambition. But ere that
There had been meetings of the cardinals
At the head quarters, moved thereto by letters,
Representations, visits, urging them
That something must be done to save the Faith
Which stood in peril from the hand of one
Who should have stayed the ark.

High Cardinals

Bourgeon in all the churches ; there red-stockinged,
And crimson-hatted, here in sober black ;
Now bald with age, now shaven to look like age
And gravity ; and mostly portly men

Of large discourse, and excellent taste in wines.
They cultivate the wisdom of the serpent,
And leave the rest to play the harmless dove,
Fulfilling thus the scripture by division
Of labour, as the modern law requires :—
You do the simple dove, as Christ enjoins,
And I will do the serpent. For the church,
As a world-kingdom, they are worldly-wise,
Subtle diplomatists, far-seeing schemers
Of crafty policy, yet often men
Who would not sacrifice a dearest friend
For its advantage, sooner than themselves
Would bleed at the same altar ; yet alas
They offer sometimes, what is holier still,
That charity which is the church's life
For the world-kingdom which they call God's church.

Men of long silence, they will seldom speak
Till they are ready to strike ; and so they held
Many a quiet meeting, letting not
A whisper of its purport from their lips,
Only they looked more grave than customary,
As they who have grave business on their hands.
In truth, they wist not what they ought to do :
The evil might be great ; but then he was
So slight a man, so inconsiderable,

Unbeneficed, unpopular ; and to break
A fly upon the wheel was apt to rouse
Unreasonable laughter, and such men
Like not such mirth.   And then as to these views—
Who could pin down a shadow to the ground,
And take its measure? who could try the notes
Of a wild bird by proper rhythmic laws ?
Or say if the wind whistled by the gamut ?
They understood not what he would be at :
A mystic, vague and unsubstantial, true
To no laws that they knew ; but they were sure
That he was vain and foolish, and would melt
Like sugar in the mouth, and be forgot
Save by some sweet-toothed children.   Let him be ;
Contempt would kill that, like a nipping frost,
Which, grown notorious, might live on a while,
And work some mischief.   They were very wise,
The portly cardinals, and yet they knew not
All that the future knew, and how the truth
Works sometimes from without as from within.

Meanwhile, he wist not what they communed of ;
None spake to him of trouble in the air,
Of ill reports, of plans to wreck his hopes,
If hope still clung to him ; nor any brother
Came in a brother's love to him, and said ;

Lo ! we will reason it together; then
God will give light perchance, and thou shalt be
Saved from much sorrow, and I shall be blessed.
They looked askance at him ; they crossed the road,
And passed on the other side ; they lifted up
Their eyes to heaven, and saw him not; or with
Broad, brazen stare they silently went on.
He noted them, but heeded not, or thought
But how the herd sweep past the stricken deer,
Or how the wild wolves, padding o'er the waste,
Eyeing a wounded comrade, think how soon
The time may come when they shall lap his blood,
Or gnaw his bones. But nothing then he knew
Of their complaints, or of the storm a-brewing ;
He only thought that people had not loved
His preaching, and would hear his voice no more ;
Else had he stayed it out to fight the fight,
For sound of trumpet and the clash of swords,
Roused in him joy of battle, even then
When hope of victory was none in him.

So, wotting not his peril, he forsook
The pulpit where they welcomed him no more—
The wandering life that, weekly, pitched its tent
In some fresh home, where children laughed and
   sang,

And all the hopes that like the ivy grew
Green about old church towers : and sat him down
In a small garret with a new-made pen.

Once they complained his sermons were like books,
Essays original and quaint, which men
Might read in print, and wisely meditate ;
And now they said his books did somewhat smack
Of homely preaching, such as long ago
Spoke to the times. He brought a sacred spirit
Unto the secular task, and called on men
To follow lofty aims and noble deeds.
Even when he laughed at fools, his mirth would be
Pitiful, and when he would edge his tool
Sharper to smite the wooden wit o' the time,
Yet was it in some cause of righteousness,
Or large humanity, that might have been
Theme of a prophet mocking at the devil.
And thus he breathed into our common life,
And round about the church, an atmosphere
That changed them both, and loosed their bonds, and wrought
As none might work within the Temple gate ;
For oft the church must learn from those without
Who paste the prophet-broadside on its wall,
Or sing their burden on the busy street.

Secular.

Who once has worn the priestly robe, and seen
  The upturned faces with their look of awe,
  As unto prophet giving forth the law
Amid the hush which, even when thought is lean,
Devoutly listens,—having erewhile been
  'Mong holy things within the altar rails,
  Is fain to hide his head, what time he fails,
And seeks his pulpit in a magazine,
Unfrocked of his own will. He shrinks with fear
  From buzzing critics carping at his wit,
And on the buried past he drops a tear,
  Until he finds the secular life is knit
And braced by freedom, and is, haply, more
Larger and fuller than his life before.

Content.

Howe'er it be with some, the broad highway
  Is better than the priestly path for me;
For when it was my task, from day to day,
To do official pieties, and pray,
  I think I might have grown a Pharisee,
Pumping my heart, when it was dry as dust,
For words of faith and hope—because I must.

Then are we at our highest, when we touch
  The Infinite and Good in worship due,
Bowing in lowly reverence to such
As we deem holiest, and trusting much
  Because the holiest is most pitying too:
Nothing so nobly human as the quest
That seeks true man in God, and there finds rest.

But he who all day handles sacred tasks,
  While his thoughts travail with the world, and he

Nor hopes to get from God the thing he asks,
Nor yet to hide from God the heart he masks
   To others—how it wounds his soul to be
Praying-machine, until the day's chief sin
Is the chief duty he has done therein !

I did not turn a Pharisee ; I fought
   Against the perils that my life beset,
And when I felt no worship, worshipped not,
And when my heart was merry, mirth I sought,
   Entangling jests like gay moths in a net,
And laughed, and made laugh, though I saw, the while,
They fancied not a priest so given to smile.

Be the road stormy, be it calm and mild,
   Yet snares are spread there, pitfalls too are dug :
The pious mother, longing that her child
May keep his white robe clean and undefiled,
   Dreams of a peaceful parsonage and snug,
Where the world comes not, neither any snare ;
Yet world and flesh and devil, too, are there.

Just past their teens, we task young souls to do
   What needs a large experience deeply-tried ;
And oft I marvel they remain so true,
Freshening the old, and bringing forth the new,
   And with the growing life still growing wide ;

For the cloud-incense of the altar hides
The true form of the God who there abides.

But now I do my work with hand and head,
   And do my worship with a separate heart;
With a good conscience earning daily bread,
And by the Heavenly Father duly fed,
   I keep the worship and the work apart;
And yet the work has worship in it too,
But willing service, not a task I do.

My heart is more at one, my soul more calm,
   My Sunday more a welcome joy to me,
Whose rest is sweetened by the folded palm,
The bended knee, and the uplifted psalm,
   While once it was a fretful troubled sea
Vexed by the thought of human praise or blame,
And only partly lit by the Great Name.

Discontent.

Sitting apart,
I hear the murmuring tide of life,
Its onward rush, and foaming strife,
    Yet bid my heart
String dainty words in fancies quaint,
    And be content.

Lying abed,
I dream, with method in my dream,
And catch up any lights that gleam
    Into my head,
And fondle a conceit, beguiled
    As by a child.

Poring o'er books,
Dingy, old volumes, by the hour,
Which only I and moths devour,
    My eyes find hooks
In each dim page, and I have peace
    In their increase.

What would I more,
Since I have dropt out of the race,
But eddy in a quiet place
            Beside the shore,
And make a play of life, and smile
        A little while?

        Yet now and then,
A something pricks me, canst thou see
The breaking waves that surge by thee;
        And has thy pen
No service, but these fancies odd,
        For man or God?

        Ah! vexing heart,
Rebellious! fain to seek the fight,
Though broken all thy force and might,
        Thou hast no part
In life, but with a patient will
        See, and be still.

Success.

I have done well, I said, for I have found
  My place in life, the work that I can do,
And in my garret, spurning the low ground,
  I can, at least, be manful, free, and true.

Nameless, I go about, and sometimes hear
  The whisper of a fame that is to come;
They wot not who I am, and I appear
  All unconcerned with that low-gathering hum.

It is like being dead, and hearing what
  Verdict of history may one day speak;
And now I laugh, and now I wonder at
  Myself, that I can be so vain and weak.

But when I think, here will I make my nest.
  Ah me! the nest unfeathered is and cold,
But sticks and thorns whereon there is no rest,
  And never love its weary wings could fold.

There is a little islet that I know,
   Blue with forget-me-nots—a lonely spot,
And no bird nestles where their gold eyes grow :
   'Tis just a home of long forget-me-not.

So lonely and so barren is my lot,
   Still dreaming where the quiet water sleeps,
To win a name that shall not be forgot;
   And that is all it either sows or reaps.

A Walk.

A clear, crisp, Autumn day.   Autumn is Scotch
And lingers lovingly among the hills,
Knee-deep in golden bracken, and golden grass
That tints the moor, what time the purple heather
Withers to brown, and golden pendants hang
On the slim, drooping birch—the golden time
Of all the Northern year.

                    You shall find spring,
Joyous with bursting life, in English lanes
Where the May-blossom wafts from straggling hedge
Its incense like a white-robed Thurifer,
While the meek violet, like a saintly soul,
Hid in a green obscurity, breathes out
Its sweets, unseen, and the pale primrose woos
The shadow at the foot of lush blue-bells.
Green are the meadows there, and green the leaves
Opening, with various shade, in chestnut whorles,
And feathery birch, and plane and beech and lime,

And late ash-bud and oak—the many tints
Like many colours, yet one flush of green
From the young life o' the year.

　　　　　　But Autumn loves
The ferny braes, the brown heath on the hills,
The lichened rocks, orange and grey and black.
The harebell and the foxglove in the shaws,
The brisk and nimble air upon the moor,
The flying cloud that scuds across the blue,
Its shadow hurrying o'er the sunlight brow
Of the still mountain, and the sleepy loch
Quivering as in a dream of coot and tern,
Or leaping trout; thither the antlered stag
Leads forth his hinds to water at the dawn:
And life is at full pitch of beauty then,
When verging to its close.

　　　　　　That Autumn day,
I wandered forth alone, in sober ways
While yet the shadow of the houses fell
Around me, and the window-eyes looked on;
Yet I was glad, for I had found my work.
And when I reached the country, and beheld
The loaded wains with the last harvest-sheaves
Led homeward, and the reapers blithe and brown,

And felt my feet among the rustling leaves
By the wayside, and watched the shining spikes
Of frost in shady nooks beside the burn,
I could not walk, but leaped, and laughed at nothings
In very joy of life ; for anything
Serves for a jest what time the heart is gay.

So on and up I went, with tireless feet,
And fertile mind suggesting victories
My pen should win for me, as the slow years
Ripened the powers which circumstance disclosed,
And critics now approved. I had the trick
Of hoping to the full, and building up
Dream-palaces, creative, out of nothing,
Collapsing into nothing at a touch
Of adverse fact ; and that day I was in
The mood to make whole worlds, with suns and stars,
And flowers and birds, and homes by love made glad.

But crossing a waste moor, where hills of slag
Rose bare, and sluggish pools were at their feet,
Where no fish swam, but red lights ever glowed,
I came upon a village mean and poor,
Which no one cared for, save to draw much wealth
From seams of coal, and veins of ironstone
That undermined it ; one long string of huts,

Ugly and dirty and monotonous;
And no bell rang there on the Sabbath morn,
And only Death e'er spoke to them of God.
Swart, stunted men were plodding from the pits,
Weary, with little lamps stuck in their caps
Instead of flower or feather; savage children
Were skulking at the doors, but none of them
Did run to meet their fathers, and be kissed
And borne home shoulder-high; the mothers, too,
Were fierce, and smiled not when the men came home,
For they were weary, and not with woman's work.
Oft had I seen the peasant from his plough
Plod slowly home, but gladdened by his girl,
Curly and sunny, chattering at his side,
And by the baby nestling on his breast,
And by the mother smiling at the door
With the milk-pail; and often watched the fisher,
Hard-faced and weather-beaten, leave his boat,
At early morn with children gambolling,
Bare-footed, on the sand, or leading him
Home in the pride of love, with the fresh spoils
Of the old sea; but such a sight as this,
So without hope or heart or any joy
I had not seen before: a place so dreary,
So God-forsaken in its ugliness,
Each house alike, the people too alike

Dismal and brutal; and the only spot
With any brightness was a drinking house
Shining with glass and brass and painted barrels.

Therewith the thought again knocked at my heart,
Urgent and loud: Was thy life given to thee
For making pretty sentences, and play
Of dainty humour for the mirthful heart
To be more merry; or to serve thy kind,
Redressing wrong? And all the long way home
That thought kept ever knocking at my heart.

Lost.

Sick, sick at heart and in despair,
Through crowded street, and quiet square
I seek my lost Love everywhere.

A while, with shamed and broken mind,
I hid from her, content to find
Her shadow nightly on the blind;

Content to hear her even-song
Go up with tremulous note or strong,
Go up the angels' hymns among,

Meanwhile I stood beneath the lamp,
And fretted on the pavement damp
At the slow Watchman's patient tramp,

Or noted where the shadows flit
On quaint old gables, or a bit
Of carving by the moonbeams lit.

The shame of failure on me lay,
And led me on a lonely way,
Hoping for dawn of a new day.

Yet now the day has come, and lo !
It is like morning creeping slow
Into a blinded house of woe.

Gone ! and she has not left a trace !
And while I haunt the silent place,
O ! I am haunted by her face.

O fool and coward ! not to see
That love, which would have trusted thee,
Must die if it distrusted be !

Change.

Ah ! to have lived at Love's high pitch,
　And then fall back on level lines
Of commonplace ! to have been rich,
　As one who ventures deep in mines,
And then to toil at hedge or ditch,
　And dream of costly fares and wines !

Gone from my life the impassioned strain
　That gave it all its tender grace,
And now its gladness is the pain
　That draws deep furrows on my face ;
But I can never stoop again
　To the dull round of commonplace.

Another passion must knit up
　These flagging energies of mine ;
No muddy water for my cup !
　But fill it full with generous wine ;
Who knows what Love is, may not sup
　On that which is not still divine.

He who was caught up, as he said,
　To the third heavens, and heard and saw
Unutterable things, would tread
　Earth after in a trance of awe,
Nor might he ever bow his head
　To bear the yoke of meaner law.

I saw the people sad and dumb,
　With none to utter their complaints,
But preached to of a world to come,
　And damned because they were not saints:
And there, I said, is work for some
　Whose heart with hunger in them faints.

𝕭𝖆𝖉 𝕿𝖎𝖒𝖊𝖘.

An evil time ! a time of deep unrest,
   And thoughts that reached out for a larger life,
When bread was dear, the poor were sore distressed
   And work was scanty, and the taxes rife.

Often, at night, I walked about the town,
   When the broad moon was silvering street and
      square,
And all the loathsome now was lovely grown,
   For only light and shadow brooded there.

Stately and fair the gabled houses rose,
   And hazy legend, or historic light
Clung to each winding stair, or murky close,
   And with the past day filled the present night.

And in a dream of history I went
   Along the centuries of pride and sin

That me o'ershadowed, till my heart was rent
  With pity of the sights I saw therein.

For often from the gloom and from the cold
  Where they lay shivering in a dusky nook,
Gaunt faces glared at me, and children told
  Their misery in a wan and wasted look.

And pest and hunger there went hand in hand,
  Invisible but strong, and some went mad,
While good men licked their lips, and looking bland
  Over their port, allowed the times were bad.

Now and Then.

One rode amid a rabble throng,
  And laid about him with a sword;
His heart was high, his hand was strong,
  Nor did he stint an angry word;
" Ho ! lurdanes, earth is full of bread,
  An ye will work for its increase,
But an ye idle here, instead,
  'Twere better that your breath should cease.
Get to the mattock and the hoe,
  The distaff and the spinning wheel;
Odd's life ! who will not work, shall know
  The bitter taste of cord or steel.
Away ! with crutch and beggar's whine !
  Away with ballad-singing rogues !
And lo ! ye shall have flesh and wine,
  And hosen warm and leathern brogues;
And there shall not be rags or debt,
  Or hunger in the land, or cold,

If ye will only dig and sweat"—
But that was in the days of old.

One looked upon a wrathful crowd
  That surged about the market square,
And with hoarse clamour cried aloud
  The spawn of Tyrants not to spare;
And from the throng he took his way
  Into a waste and desert land,
In loneliness to brood and pray,
  And bring back order and command.
Then coming from the desert place,
  Again the market-square he trod,
With shining glories in his face,
  And laws that had the seal of God:
"Behold," he said, "the gods command
  That ye shall keep these statutes good,
And they will give you fruitful land
  To dwell in, and ye shall have food."
And they had faith, and writ the laws
  In letters large of gleaming gold,
To order every plea and cause—
  But that was in the days of old.

But now this pinched and sunk-eyed mob,
  'Tis work they ask the Powers to give,

Hating to filch or steal or rob,
   Ashamed to beg that they may live.
But silent is the clicking loom,
   And silent too the birring wheel,
The flaming forge is quenched in gloom,
   The mill is grinding little meal.
The ships are rotting in the dock,
   The cage hangs listless o'er the mine,
The hammer rings not on the rock,
   The spade rusts on the unfinished line,
And gladly would they toil and sweat,
   Without the taste of cord or steel,
And gladly keep the order set
   By any law the gods could seal.
But I have only tongue and pen,
   And neither force nor faith to hold
My way among the sons of men
   As they did in the days of old.

How we did it.

Erewhile our forefathers, hating oppression,
   Sware a great oath that their blood they would
      spill,
New-hefted scythe, issued plea and Confession,
   Scoured the old musket, and took to the hill.

Loomed in the front of them scaffold and halter,
   Hunger and weariness, battle and death,
Only the mists of the mountain for shelter,
   Only the raven to watch their last breath.

Times were heroic then ; e'en the slow peasant
   Felt his heart swell 'mid the trumpets and spears ;
And if our commonplace way is more pleasant,
   Yet we have lost the great soul of those years.

We held monster-meetings, signed tons of petitions,
   And snowed all the country with leaflets and tracts,
Setting forth all our desires and conditions,
   And bristling with arguments, figures, and facts.

With weekly pennies, and working committees,
  And secretaries, and printing large,
We knit together the towns and cities,
  And rallied the battle, and made our charge.

Heroes we were not; for they were not wanted;
  Power now must yield what the people demand;
But sometimes I laughed as our doings we vaunted,
  The work was so common, the words were so
    grand.

Yet what have the ages been slowly achieving,
  By slings, bows and arrows, and muskets and
    swords,
But just that we now should be peacefully weaving
  Far mightier spells by the virtue of words?

Storm-Birds.

O creatures of the storm !
Shrill birds that scream but when the shrill winds
blow,
And fish of monstrous form,
Which the long rollers on the sand-beach throw,
And with the tangled wrack drift to and fro ;
You well I know.

O creatures of the storm !
That creep out of your holes to meet the rain,
Foul toad and slug and worm,
And to your proper dark return again,
When the sun shines, and merry birds are fain
To sing amain !

Yet the storm also brings
The Master to the helm the ship to guide,
And deftly trim her wings,
And shape her course amid the wind and tide,
And so the best and worst are side by side,
While storms abide.

Rumour.

Open-mouthed Rumour ran from street to street,
　Telling of flour devoured by rats and mice;
Telling of old stacked corn by wet and heat
　Wasted, while waiting for a famine-price;

Telling of fortunes speculators made
　Out of the miseries of the hapless poor;
Telling of mothers starved and lying dead,
　While babies gnawed their breasts upon the floor;

Telling of men devouring grass and hay
　To stay the hunger that devoured their bones;
Telling how gamesome children now would play
　At funerals only on the paving stones;

Telling how soldiers did their sabres whet,
　And kept their horses saddled day and night,
And primed their muskets when the people met,
　Ready to quench in blood the cause of right;

Telling of speakers threatened for true words ;
  Telling of lawyers framing treason-pleas ;
Telling of harsh things done by angry lords ;
  Telling of statesmen who were ill at ease.

Many-tongued Rumour had a busy time,
  And men were greedy for the tales she bore,
And when she told of madness, sin, or crime,
  The worse the story they believed the more !

O foolish world, be-rumoured of thy wits !
  How had a spark then set thee in a blaze
Amid thy heats and chills and trembling fits,
  And turned to grief the glory of those days !

Triumph.

Upon a day of triumph some will shout,
   And set the bells a-ringing in the steeple,
   And fountains spouting wine for all the people,
And lights in all the windows round about.

They must have noise of cracker, squib, and gun,
   And at the market-cross with loud hurrahing,
   And shaking hands, and bands of music playing,
They will proclaim that now the day is won.

For me, I went home with a quaint old book,
   And shut me in to have a long night's reading;
   That was my payment, for my soul was needing
Still waters in a restful, quiet nook.

Well; each man has his way, and this was mine;
   I could not care for fizzing squibs and crackers,
   Hallooing crowds, and empty boastful talkers
Made eloquent by vanity and wine.

Tramp, tramp, I heard them marching here and there,
  With strutting bagpipe, or with noisy drumming;
  And when I hoped that surely calm was coming,
Fresh clamours rose with rockets in the air.

And at my door they paused a while, and gave
  A ringing cheer that set my heart a-beating,
  And flung their caps on high with kindly greeting,
And slowly ebbed back like a broken wave.

As they were glad, I let them have their way;
  As I was glad, I took my own good pleasure;
  And while they bawled and shouted without
      measure,
I read old Chronicles till break of day.

Endings.

Note.

Rarely is life compact into a plot
Carefully laid, with deepening interest,
Dramatic unities, and characters
Entangled in a tragic Fate that works
To a foredoomed catastrophe, and melts
All hearts with pity. Unto most of us
There comes no great event for winding up
The story—only chapters broken short,
And, one by one, the snapping of some thread,
Once twined with ours, making it full and strong,
And now by loss enfeebling it, till life,
Grown thin and lonely, tapers to its close
With lessening interest: a tragic tale,
And yet without a grand catastrophe.
So Raban judged it, when he summed his days
In broken ends whereat the once full life

Oozed out, and he went on his way alone,
Making no loud complainings, blaming none
But himself only, and seeing good in all—
Some touch of grace which shewed that they were
    human,
Or broken link which proved them once divine.

Retrospect.

The traveller in the desert lone
  Looks back, regretful oft, to think
  Of the sweet wells where he could drink,
Ere Fate had lured, or driven him on
  Into a wan and wasted land
  Of Wadys where the streams are sand.

And wistfully I, too, look back
  From life, successful as they say,
  That has no water by the way ;
And it is water that I lack,
  And there was water for my thirst,
  When failure of my hope was worst.

There is no life so commonplace
  But, if you search it, you shall find
  A secret chamber of the mind,
Enshrining some fair sainted face,
  Where worship still is done with tears
  That freshen the grey dusky years.

That was its living water once,
  Sweet-singing ever by the way,
  And gleaming through its darkest day,—
The glory of its young Romance :
  But O, the desert wastes that spread
  Where Love lives on, and Hope is dead !

Omen.

A fair white dove came to my window sill
    In the faint morning light,
Preening its feathers with a pale pink bill
    Daintily in my sight,
Nodding its head with pretty curtsey still
    To left and right,
    And then took flight.
O fair, white dove, I meant to thee no ill;
    Why did'st thou then take fright,
    And vanish into night?

The Public Meeting.

I stood up to speak. At my back was a score
  Of broadcloth respectables solemnly stewing,
For the vast hall was filled from the roof to the floor,
And they swarmed, thick as bees, at each window
    and door;
    And I knew, at a glance, that a storm was
    a-brewing
      For my sure undoing.

Yet I stood up to speak. Almost under my feet,
  With pencil and note-book, were newspaper men;
Some staid-looking working lads kept the first seat,
Then students and snobs and the cads of the street,
    With a woman, perhaps, for each threescore and ten,
      And a child, now and then.

I was not ta'en aback, in the least, though I saw
  That the meeting was packed with a loud senseless
    mob,
And standing near by, was a Limb-o'-the-Law
Who rubbed his sleek chin with a vulture-like claw,

And a grin of conceit at the well-managed job,
    Which made my pulse throb.

So I stood up to speak. What a greeting I had !
  They hooted, yelled, whistled, and cat-called and
      groaned,
Hissed, jeered at me, howled; cried "His throat
      sure is bad !"
"Cough it up !" "Try an orange !" and "Was I
      not glad
  To address my dear friends ?" Then they hooted
      and moaned,
      And sang and intoned.

Still I held my ground stoutly; replied as I could;
  At times ready-witted, and then got a laugh,
But always good-humoured : I thought that their
      mood
Would change by and by, when they saw that I stood
  With unruffled temper, and bore all the chaff
      Of that stormy riff-raff.

I had often stood there with a ringing hurrah !
  That greeted each hit; and I would not be beat,
As I watched that long Limb-o'-the-Law looking
      grey

While he signalled his Claque; so I stood there at
    bay,
  Though the Kentish fire rung out from three
    thousand feet
      With a fierce dust and heat.

But scanning their faces, I saw that the most
  Were brainless or beery, or big-jowled with low
Brute foreheads, and felt that our cause must be lost
With a white-chokered Chairman as pale as a ghost,
  And those broad-cloth respectables, ranged in a row,
    Full of dismal dumb-show.

Never mind; I would try; I had lungs that would
    shout
  Like a boatswain's, and ring with the storm at
    its height;
And I knew people liked me; and half of the rout
Was the clamour of friends who would have me
    hold out,
  Though I had to gesticulate till the daylight
    Broke on that stormy night.

So I plucked up my courage, and threw back the hair
  From my brow, scanned the Lawyer from top
    down to toe,

Who gave back my gaze with an impudent stare;
Then I nodded, and smiled to my friends here and
    there,
  While I watched the dim crowd as it swayed to
    and fro,
      Seeming wilder to grow.

Now, a score of cocks crew as to welcome the day,
  Then a wild caterwauling of cats in the dark
Through the galleries ran; then a donkey would
    bray,
Or dogs yelped and howled in a horrible way,
  As if all the creatures shut up in the Ark
      Came to yell, scream, or bark.

After that rose a chorus of " God save the Queen,"
  With a tramping of boots keeping time. How
    the dust
Rose in clouds until hardly a face could be seen!
How they roared themselves hoarse! What a
    coughing between
  Each verse as they sang out of tune! for they must
      Clear their throats of the rust.

It was all in the programme, of course; so I stood
  And patiently edged in a word here and there,

Now lost in the clamour, now half-understood,
Now caught by the grinning reporters, now good,
  But as often bad ; and I did not much care;
        It was spent on the air.

Should I try any longer ?   What hope there to speak
  Words of reason to men who all reason eschew ?
Highest truths to such ears were but Hebrew and
      Greek,
And logic no more than the doors when they creak,
  And pathos like wind in a cranny that blew ;
        And they'd laugh at it too.

Leave the fools to the fate they are fain to provoke !
  They will know what it is in the coming distress,
When they've damped down the furnace, and cleared
      off the smoke,
And emptied the yards, and begin then to croak
  That taxes grow bigger as wages grow less,
        And the hard times press !

Let them be till the workshop is empty and still,
  And the clock on the wall does not wag any more,
And the fire does not burn, though the winter is chill,
And there's nothing to pawn, and there's nothing to
      fill

The pale and pinched children that cry at the door,
　　Or squat on the floor !

Just then, looking down, my eye caught in the aisle
　A white oval face sweetly turned up to mine,
Lips parted in eagerness, tipped with a smile
As the great purple eyes beamed upon me a while,
　Or flashed on the crowd with an anger divine
　　That warmed me like wine.

'Twas the face I had loved in the House in the
　　Square !
　Just that look it had worn when her soul was
　　inspired,
As we read of the heroes of old who could dare
The rage of the Demos, when madness was there,
　Or wrath of the gods, when their anger was fired,
　　And their patience expired.

She had haunted my dreams, as I struggled to rise,
　She had cheered me in vision, what time I had
　　failed,
And now there she sat, and I saw in her eyes
The fond love of youth without let or disguise,¶
　Till she wist that I saw it, and trembled and quailed,
　　And the glowing face paled.

Then I said in my heart: No, I will not be beat;
  She shall not regret to have trusted me so;
I have stood for an hour in the roar and the heat,
I will stand till the day dash its light at my feet;
  But she shall not go home with her faith sinking
    low
        In the dear long ago.

That moment a lull came, and stir near the door;
  Some were weary of shouting, some went out for
    beer;
So I slipt in a joke, setting some in a roar,
Then a story that tickled their humour; that o'er,
  For one that still hissed, there were twenty cried
    Hear!
        And my way was all clear.

But my blood now was up: Ware! my Limb-o'-the-
  Law!
  Who would drown voice of reason with clamour
    and shout;
With the laugh on my side now, at each hit I saw
His cheek grow more livid, his vulture-like claw
  Twitch and clutch at the chin it went feeling
    about,
        As my wrath was poured out.

" "Twas the way of all Tyrants to gag our free
    speech,
  And the sign of a bad cause to shrink from debate;
Let them look to their freedom when those who
    should preach
Law and order, brought rowdies whom nothing could
    teach,
    Beered up to the lips, to roar like a spate,
        Drowning truth which they hate."

Then I tossed him aside, and took up the great
    theme
  Of Justice and Peace, till they thrilled at my
    words ;
Yet I saw but the flush on her face, and the gleam
Of the great purple eyes, as she drank in the stream
    That reasoned against the unreason of swords
        For man's law and the Lord's.

" There was a wild madness abroad in the air,
  A longing for war which the rulers had nursed ;
They had roused up the wild beast that still had
    his lair
In the civilized heart, without cause that would bear
    The quarrel of nations ; and with a blood-thirst
        The land was accursed."

L

Then I sat down at last, 'mid a ringing Hurrah !
  And kindly pet names, and a hum of content,
As the motion was carried ; and hasting away,
I watched by the great door, and stood in the grey
  Watery light of the moon, till the last of them went—
        Very weary and spent.

I peered at each veiled face, but met not her gaze,
  Poked my head in each bonnet, but she was not
        there,
Saw white fingers point at me, heard whispered praise,
And remarks on my pluck from a cab or a chaise ;
  But my heart sank within me in very despair,
        And I heard unaware.

I had seen her once more, but to lose her again,
  Through that storm she had burst like a sunblink
        on me ;
And the joy of young Love flushed my heart and
        my brain,
Like a fresh aftermath breathing sweet after rain,
  With all the birds singing on bush and tree—
        And now where was she ?

Could my eyes have played false ? Could there be
  a mistake ?

No; there was none else with those wonderful
    eyes,
And there was none else in the world that could
    make
My heart so to flutter and beat for her sake,
    And there was none else could my soul so
    surprise
        With old memories.

.   .   .   .

Later on in the evening I sat by the fire,
    Alone, and in silence, my heart very low,
All the triumph gone out in a longing desire,
As I saw the moon pale, and her glory expire
    In a dull drizzling rain falling steady and slow,
        When the wind ceased to blow.

I mused on the past; on the House in the Square,
    On the hope that had clung to me all the long
        years,
Unspoken, 'mid struggle and failure and care;
And now in the hour when I felt I might dare,
    She had come—she had gone—as a phantom
    appears;
        And my eyes swam in tears.

Then there came to my door just the faintest of
    taps,
  Like the sound of small fingers that timidly knock ;
"Come in ;" I look up, and some moments elapse
In stillness ; and then again two or three raps,
    But never a movement of latch or lock
        On the dull silence broke.

"O the housemaid, of course ; she is wanting to
      bed ;
  No wonder, poor drudge !" So I opened the door ;
"No supper to-night, Jane," I wearily said :
But it was not the housemaid I saw: in her stead
    Was the white oval face of the sweet days of yore,
        Gazing at me once more.

I breathed a long breath : was I dreaming ? or
    what ?
  Tongue-tied there I stood, as if bound by a spell :
Then she dropped me a curtsey ; still stood on the
    mat ;
Called me "Sir ;" and "Felt sure I had seen where
    she sat ;
  And she could not go home without coming to
    tell
        I did bravely and well.

" Her husband was waiting her out in the street ;
　And O she was proud to have heard me that
　　　night ;
Had her mother but witnessed my triumph complete,
Who had always believed in me !" Then, with a
　　　sweet
　Smile, glided away like a ghost out of sight,
　　　　Ere my senses came right.

I had been quite bemazed : she had curtseyed
　　　to me !
　Called me " Sir "—me that would have gone down
　　　at her feet,
And grovelled to kiss her wet frock, or to be
Trod upon, for it had been an honour if she
　Should use me to carpet the stones on the street.
　　　　And go dainty and neat !

Did she speak of a husband ? I groaned at the
　　　thought,
　Sick at heart—I who loved so had never once
　　　kissed
Her lips, save in dreams of a happier lot ;
And now all my loving and waiting had brought—
　What was it ?—a vision that passed ere I wist,
　　　　Like a vanishing mist.

I rushed out of door, up the street, and then down,
   But saw not a form in the dull drizzling rain,
And heard not a footfall : the watch of the town
Flashed his bull's-eye upon me from toe up to crown :
   " No, no one had passed ; " so I crept home again
      In wonder and pain.

She had gone from my life, and its light was all gone ;
   She had gone from my life, and I saw her no more ;
Drip, drip ! let it pelt !—it was eerie and lone ;
So was I ; and my heart lay within me like stone ;
   And I cared not although the slow pitiless pour
      Should drip evermore.

Misgiving.

Has he done wrong, who, as the years go past,
　In loneliness, knowing it all in vain,
　As he has loved before, to love again,
Brings to his home another bride at last?

Tender and kind, he cherishes his mate,
　More tenderly the more he feels that she
　Gets not the perfect love which ought to be
The guerdon and the bliss of wife's estate.

For while he gently kisses her fond lips,
　It is another face that meets his gaze;
　And he is stung by words of love or praise
Which the truth known would darken with eclipse.

O sorrow and shame! that, while he lies beside
　The trusting one, he in the silence hears
　His heart throb for the love of other years,
And calm to her whom he has made his bride.

Remorse.

Alas ! she did not long with me abide,
    But pining slowly,
Like waning moon, she faded by my side
    With melancholy,
    And in our fifth spring, died.

I lifted up the face-cloth from her face ;
    Upon its beauty,
Stony and still, yet lay the tender grace
    Of love and duty,
    And patient sorrow's trace.

O heart, I said, that gavest me all thy wealth,
    Of love's rich treasure,
And now by open service, now by stealth,
    Were't fain to pleasure
    My sickness or my health ;

O faithful heart ! and yet thou had'st from me
    Observance only :

And still thy wistful, hungry look would be
    Like one who, lonely,
  Gazes far out at sea—

Gazes far out to catch the hoped-for sail
    Film the horizon,
But only ocean fretting in the gale
    She sets her eyes on,
  And hears the sea-mew wail.

I gave thee what I had; but that was not
    What love expected ;
And when the fond heart for a fond heart sought,
    Thy love detected
  The emptiness it got.

I took thy gold, and gave thee but my brass;
    Though deep indebted,
When thou would'st look for more, I let thee pass,
      Or even fretted
  That thou should'st sigh alas !

I gave thee kisses, but my kiss was cold,
    And dainty dresses,
I did not grudge thee jewels set in gold
    For thy caresses,
  As if they had been sold.

But that alacrity which doth prevent
        Our wishes even,
That pleasure which on pleasing still is bent,
        That was not given,
    Which might thy soul content.

Thy heart for love was longing, and mine had
        No love to give it—
A ruin haunted by a memory sad,
        That would not leave it
    Though truth and duty bade.

I called it sentimental, silly, wrong ;
        But yet it nestled
The closer, and I think it grew more strong
        The more I wrestled,
    And I did wrestle long.

O pardon ! that I was not true to thee ;
        I tried to will it,
And then the Past arose and wailed in me,
        Nor could I still it
    More than the sounding sea.

Ah ! to be true to thee, and false to her !—
        I could not do it ;

Yet to be false to thee a baseness were,
   And I should rue it
  In life and character !

So life is ravelled almost ere we wot;
   And with our vexing
To disentangle it, we make the knot
   But more perplexing,
  Embittering our lot.

Farewell, true heart; my sorrow stirs in me
   With no self-pity,
But shamed and self-condemning. But I see
   The Holy City
  Opening its gates to thee—

Opening its gates to shew thee all the truth
   And all the folly;
The secret of the sorrow of thy youth,
   And melancholy
  Which touches me with ruth.

Farewell ; while thou hadst being here and breath,
   The truth was hidden,
But now before the majesty of death
   My soul, God-bidden,
  Speaks out its better faith.

After Dinner.

Returned from Ballarat, where he had found
Gold nuggets in the early rush, and more
Golden experience, Martin Lusk, one day,
Bearded and bronzed, dropt in upon the quiet
Where I with treasured books—mine ancient friends—
Was communing. At first, I knew him not,
But soon the name recalled a form, a face
From the dim past, that might perhaps have grown
Into this son of Anak. So we fell
A-talking, and I found his mind well stored
With fresh quaint pictures of that Digger-life
Fighting with Death and Fortune, gambling, drinking,
Thieving and pistolling, in dirt and splendour,
Brutal-heroic, yet with touching gleams
Of human tenderness, and gradual sway
Of Law that, self-evolved, yet mastered self,
And rough-shaped that wild chaos. I could see
This keen observer was a thinker too,
Patient and tolerant, with the stuff in him

For building up an empire.   Being lonely
In his hotel, and so conversible,
I made him promise he would dine with me.

Reluctant he agreed, reluctant came,
And sat uneasy and silent, changed as much
From the clear-sighted man I met at noon
As from the bright-eyed youth of early days.
Lusk, as a lad, was bold and confident,
An only son, spoilt by a doating mother,
Spoilt, too, by sisters proud of him, even spoilt
By admiration of his college mates
For a rich nature foremost in all games,
Foremost in studies, and in ready speech,
And yet not greatly spoilt by all their spoiling,
Just frank and bold and sure of his position.
But now he sat there, like a bashful girl
At her first ball, blushing, and hardly spoke
Save yea and nay, until we were alone.

Then I : What ails you, Martin ?   What is wrong ?
Have we done aught to vex you, that you sit
Dumb as a moulting raven ?   My home-bred girls,
Untravelled, when they heard that you were coming,
Donned their best muslins, and their gayest ribbons,
Meaning to show their best, and talk their best,

And listen at their best. For they were all
Eager to hear of pouchëd Kangaroos,
And duck-billed quadrupeds, and great Emus
Piling their eggs amid the sandy scrub,
Black-fellows, and the pig-tailed Chinamen,
Bush-rangers, and the cradling and the crushing,
And nugget-finding in the deep-delved loam,
And other strange adventures of your life,
As they romanced it; for the less they know,
The more their fancy bubbles up and glitters.
Yet there you sat, and stammered curt replies
As frightened at their feather-heads. They'll vow
That my old friends are stupid as myself:
And O. if they had seen what you had seen !
If girls might only do what men may do,
They would have tongues to tell it.

      Nothing ails me,
He said; I did not know I was so rude:
But coming from our rough unmannered life
Among a group of happy girls like yours,
Free in their innocence, is like the passing,
Sudden, from dark into the blaze of noon;
Your eyes blink and are blinded. It is long
Since I have sat beside pure-hearted maids,
And listening to their words, my thoughts went back
To dear old times; I seemed to hear again,

Dreamily, echoes of old fireside mirth,
And chatter of the table. Was I rude?
I did not mean it. Half I envied you,
And half I feared that some ill-sorted word
Of mine might break the charm. 'Tis strange that we
May wallow with the swine, and grunt with them,
Till those fair customs which were native to us,
Grown unfamiliar, make us pick our steps
In fear and silence.

                    Laughing, I replied
It was the last thing I'd have dreamed, that he
Who, like a young Greek strong in grace of mind
And manhood, used to fire young maiden fancies,
While he himself was cool amid their tremors,
Should sit abashed with home-bred girls.

                            This led
To talk of College days and College friends—
How one was mossing in a drowsy manse;
Another loud on platforms, half a priest,
Half demagogue, who played on prejudice
With evil skill; another, wigged and gowned,
Bade fair to lead the Bar, and win the Bench;
And this, a kindly humorist whose speech
Was charming to the lecture-hearing Public:
Some doctored west-end patients, some the east;
While some were dead, and others worse than dead,

Turning up, now and then, in rusty black
And dirty linen, rubicund of face,
Begging a paltry loan. We wondered much
How the world-school reversed the classic school,
And jumbled reputations ; fancied what
If, by some chance, another pair were met,
That evening, in the bush beneath the Cross,
Or Indian dusky city, or London Club,
They might of us be saying, as we of these ;
Then we sat silent, musing for a space.

Then he : What came of Muriel Lumisden ?
You used to haunt the widow's house, I think,
With the fair daughters. What a flirt she was !
And how she kept a score of silly lads
Dangling about her, every one quite sure
He was the favoured, and the rest were gulls !
Flirting came natural to her ; you could see it
In every movement, every dainty curl
And fold of her black hair, in every tone,
And glance and turn of the eyebrows, and in all
The gesture of her lithe and supple beauty.
To flirt was in the marrow of her bones ;
Even as a child she'd make eyes to her doll ;
And just to keep her hand in, I have known her
Beam on the butcher's boy a winning glance

That sent him halfway heavenward to his calves.
And yet there have been times when she has seemed
A noble creature to me, all compact
Of womanly grace, and heart that answered true
To every noblest impulse, and inspired
High-souled enthusiasm, till I have felt
I could have been content to do some deed
That she would smile upon, and then to die,
Keeping that smile for ever. How she fooled us !
Yet O how beautiful she was ! those eyes
Melting with tenderness, or flashing scorn
At any baseness, and those lips for all
Emotions eloquent ! But such a flirt !

Hearing this passionate strain, which had been lying
In wait for opportunity, I think,
All through the night's discourse, the storm broke out
So unexpectedly, I called to mind
Some passages between them, and the talk
That buzzed about them when he went away—
How people said that she had wrecked a life
Of splendid promise; how they pitied him,
All blaming her, and yet they nothing knew,
But that he loved, and that he loved in vain,
And that he wooed, but had not won her hand,
And that he rushed off, when his luck had failed,

M

To the far ends o' the earth.   Musing on this,
And on his passionate upbraiding now,
I marvelled how he kept this open wound
Rankling, unhealed, through all the changeful years,
Wronging himself and her.   What should I say?
Better the old pain Custom helps to bear?
Or the fresh anguish which the truth will give?
So my mind balanced it.   But I resolved;
Better the truth restoring the old faith,
Even though it shame and break him.
       Then I said:
Poor Muriel! so you have not heard her story:
And you have held her but a wanton flirt,
Heartless, and with her beauty breaking hearts;
So high an inspiration, yet so mean
A nature too!   Well; maybe; only flirts
Have not such souls as make one feel one's-self
Little beside them—as a rule, at least.
And Muriel who, you say, was such a flirt,
Rebuked me by the greatness of her soul,
And of her sorrow.   Shall I tell you what,
I fear, may pain alike by gain and loss?

Then he: What mean you?   Loss is long since lost,
And gain can never be from her to me.
You knew her not as I did.   What remains

When bubbles burst i' the hand? not even the glitter.
Is she a maiden still, and fancy-free?
Why, so am I, and free of her for ever.
Is she a widow? I should gain a loss,
Indeed, to be her second. Is that your riddle?
Or is she mated to a life-long sorrow?
What else could come of such a way as hers?

Listen, I said: You were not gone a year
When one came from New Zealand, who had been
Sheep-farming in a patriarchal way
To win his Rachel, long since won to love,
What time the lad was schooling at her Father's.
A fine young fellow, cheery as the spring
At pairing time, when songs are in the woods,
And in the air, and in the furze and broom;
Manly and kindly too, and full of trust
In Muriel, though she went on as before
With speech and smile and charm of witching beauty,
And winning manner; but behind the scenes
They knew each other, and he knew her love
Was his alone. He liked to see her worshipped,
Being proud of her, and sure of her. Perhaps
She liked, too, being worshipped; who can tell?
You say she was a flirt—and you knew best:
I tell but what I saw. Well, by and by,

The wedding came, and every one was bidden,
And every one was there of her old friends,
Or lovers, and the joy was very great.
But from that moment she became to all
The staidest matron, with a kindly distance
And dignity of noble womanhood,
Hedging her round. It seems that he had said
She must not play the nun, when he was gone,
And sit apart, as ticketed " Engaged,"
But take life as it came, like other girls,
Not making him, far off, a haunting fear,
A shadow on the sunshine of her days,
But being joyous in her truth to him,
Which was her freedom; so would he be glad,
Thinking her glad.

          A happier man than he
Now there was none, nor yet a brighter home
Than that she made him, with her pretty ways,
And pretty babes, and large intelligence.

Psha ! he broke in; of course, a blessed pair
Of doves; the usual fashion; haunted they
By no regrets for broken lives, the while
They twain sat cooing. Pass to something else;
It does not interest me—'tis all so common.
Tell me about yourself, for you alone

Have made a name that even our wild lads
Had kindly in their mouths.
                                    But I : Nay, you
Must hear me out, seeing I have begun—
There came a day when he must go again
Back to his flocks : there had been summer droughts
That parched the grass, and heavy winter snows,
When many weaklings perished in the drift ;
And over all the Colony a cloud
Hung lowering, for the Maori threatened war,
Fenced his strong Pah, and sent his fighting men
To waste and burn and stealthily to kill.
So they went off together : at first he urged
That she should stay behind, for war was ill
To face, with wife and children in the rear
Plucking your heart, and savages in front
Who had no law or pity : she would find
It hard to be alone i' the bush, and quake
For her dear babes at every whispering wind,
Or rustling leaf, dreading the cunning foe.
A year or two, and all would right itself,
And he would sell his run, and live at home
With nought to do but love her. Thus he spake
In reason and right feeling, though his heart
Was sore at parting. But she answered him
With the great heart which used to fire our youth :

If war were coming, he would better fight
That his wife bound his sword on, and was near
To bind his wounds, and to call pitying thoughts
Up in his mind, amid the storm of wrath,
For savage women wailing in their Kraals;
Exile would be to part her now from him,
And home was just where he was; for herself,
She would not lose a year of happiness,
Nor give a year of loneliness to him,
For worlds; and life was there where duty was,
Not elsewhere; and their God was also there,
I' the bush as in the city. So they sailed
In a great ship crowded with emigrants,
That down the Mersey dropt with favouring breeze,
And ringing cheers upon the crowded wharf,
And blinding tears upon the crowded deck,
And many hopes, and many a sad regret.

But in the night she, bearing down the Channel
Through a thick fog, struck on a hidden rock,
Yet in a quiet sea. The sailors thought,
With the next tide she would be floated off;
And many went to sleep again, scarce heeding
Whether she sank or swam, if they might rest,
And sleep and dream of home. But by and by,
The Master grew uneasy, muttered somewhat

Of cranky ships that scarce would float in ponds,
Dry-rotten in the docks—of useless boats
That were but painted tinder; and one heard him
Murmur a prayer for wife and babes, the while
He paced the deck alone, and resolute
Issued his orders. Then a whisper went,
Gloomy, that she was leaking, and would soon
Break up amid-ships; but as yet there was
No panic, for the land was not far off.
But as the day broke, eerie, on the fog,
The timbers 'gan to crack, and great seams yawned,
And with the rushing tide the terror rose.
Then hands unhandy loosed the painted boats,
And swamped them; and from near four hundred
　　　throats
A cry rose to high heaven—a pitiful cry
Of anguish that might touch the heart of Fate,
As to and fro they reeled, and wrung their hands.

Muriel stood with her husband and her babes,
Calm, on the poop. She saw the dim grey sea
Deceitful, and the shore loomed through the mist,
Uncertain, for there was no gleam of light
From fisher's hut or farm; a lone waste land
Of unthrift and neglected husbandry,
Where neither glebe nor sea was harvested.

'Then, holding fast her little ones, her face
Just a shade paler—it was always pale—
She said in a low voice : You can swim, Malcolm ;
The shore is near, I think a sandy shore
By the dull thud o' the waves ; could you not save
Some mother and her child, setting example
Others might follow ?   O we're not afraid,
My little ones and I ; God cares for us ;
And you will come too ere the danger comes.
The Captain says the ship will float an hour
At least, and it is misery to see
Those faces, and to hear the bitter cries.
Nay, not us first ! but speak a word to them,
And show them what to do ; we can be still,
But they are frantic, and their madness works
Their ruin ; we will wait in patience here.
Try, dearest ; you are strong and brave ; but yet
Be not too bold, your life is all to us.
O can God hear that cry, and help them not ?

Fain would he still have borne her first to land
With her two boys, but that she would not hear of.
Thrice, therefore, from the ship he swam ashore,
Burdened with child or mother, or with both ;
And thrice again he left to seek the ship,
Strong swimmer borne up by his work of pity,

For nature makes the brave heart strong to save.
And at the next time, Muriel from the poop
Lowered the children to his loving arms,
Her great eyes swimming in the pride of him
And love of them, until she hardly saw
Aught else, or heard a warning cry; and then,
Just as he, confident and cheerful, held
The children, and was waiting for her coming,
A spar fell from the falling mast, and smote
Him smiling up to her, and with a cry,
And flinging up his arms, before her eyes
He sank with their two babes.   Yet she was spared
A tragic agony by tragic fact,
For the great ship that instant brake in twain.
In death they were not separate; and soon
The quiet waters, smiling in the sun,
Rippled where they had been.   .
      Here Martin rose,
Pale as a ghost, and shivering as a reed,
Alone in withered Autumn, that is smote
By sudden gust of storm.
       And I have railed,
He gasped, at such an one as this ! for years
Have rated her, and called her worthless flirt
Who broke my worthless life ! have quoted her
To lads who still had faith in truth and love,

To cure them of their folly, and have held
Myself the one wise man ! O God, my God !
To have so wronged the woman that I loved !
To have so 'stranged my nature from all love !
To have so grossly slandered truth and love !
God's beautiful one !—My broken life, forsooth !
O poor self-pitying fool ! But lost is lost ;
And this is gain though it be shame to me,
Sorrowful gain by loss of evil thought,
And love restored ; yet better so restored
Amid my self-contempt, than as before
Blurred in my self-conceit. O Muriel, yet
I loved you through it all—a hateful love !
But clinging to thee, seeing no one worthy
Save thee, and thee unworthy, and with this
So worthless love still wronging thee !—Good night !
I thank you, friend ; yes, you have done me good ;
There's healing in such sorrow ; but to-night
I could not meet your girls ; I have done wrong
Unto all women by my thoughts, and dare not
Look in their eyes. And I must be alone :
Beg my forgiveness ; I must be alone ;
God help me ! I will to the old seashore,
And hear the dull waves thudding on the sand
As my thoughts break in me. O Muriel !—
With that he gave my hand a silent grip,

And gulping something down, pulled his hat low
Over his brows, and strode into the dark.

Alone, alone, I fell into a strain
    Of musing melancholy,
Recalling, with keen sense of shame and pain,
A man whom, living, I had reckoned vain,
    And to his calling holy
Untrue, until I read, with blinding tears
Which give clear sight, the story of his fears
And clingings unto God through weary years,
    Till peace came slowly
    To him grown meek and lowly.

And I have sinned against a soul, I said,
    Noble and good and true,
Whom God has gathered with the blessed dead,
And put the crown of glory on his head,
    And I am humbled too :
But by this shame, O Lord, thou teachest me,
He only walks aright who walks with Thee,
Meek, in the judgments of that Charity
    Which unto all is due,
    And never heart shall rue.

Stray Leaves.

Note.

Riding one day from Cairnoch on the hill
Across the moor, Dick Ostler flicked the ear
Of the brown mare, then jerked his elbow and thumb
To bid me note a rounded hill that lay
Well to the setting sun, grotesquely planted
With various forest trees—oaks, elms, and pines.
Upon the lower slopes were hollow squares
Just touching each a corner of the other,
And in the bay between, a single tree
Or little group, but on the heights above
Were solid masses, interspersed with some
Carelessly strewn about.

                 " Queer woodcraft that,"
Dick Ostler said ; "and yet I planted them.
You see, our last lord went a soldiering
In his hot youth, and brave enough he looked,
Though not much of a soldier—that needs headpiece;
And coming home he took to forestry
When I was in my teens. He said the Duke
Ordered the battle so at Waterloo,

And I must range them like his regiments,
Though all the country laughed at me.   Ere long
He went to Parliament and made a speech,
Although he was no Senator—that too
Needs headpiece; and he wanted me to plant
The Speaker and the members as they sat
To hear his oratory; but that I would not;
And that was how I took to horses, sir,—
Me who had lived in forests all my days,
And loved the trees, and knew their forms and times,
And every sound of every swinging branch
When the wind blew; and I must handle brutes!
Because my lord would have it he must serve
The nation fighting, though he was no soldier,
Or parliamenting, though he could not speak!
If he had just believed that God made some
To stay at home, and see the farming done,
And look to cottar's houses, and consort
With neighbours on the market-days!   But he,
He was my lord, and must as other lords,
And would have writ his foolish life in trees
Sprawling about the estate for folk to laugh at.
That's how I took to horses."   Then he gave
The Brown another flick on the left ear,
And screwed his face into a look of strong
Disgust.

I laughed, and vowed I did not wonder
At his displeasure ; but he set me musing :
Had not my old friend writ his life likewise,
Planting along its paths a little border
Of verses like so many daisy-flowers
In memory of his failures. He was not
A preacher, though he writ some sermons, nor
A politician, though he joined a party,
And did it service. Better sure for him
Had he believed God makes some men to write,
And brighten life with gleams of better life,
Or oil its wheels with humour. So it seemed
To me, when turning over articles,
Reviews and Essays, and the odds and ends
Of verse that lay among them all confused,
Whereof some samples follow, like the thrums
Remaining when the web has been wrought out.

N

Miss Penelope Leith.

Last heiress she of many a rood,
  Where Ugie winds through Buchan braes—
A treeless land, where beeves are good,
  And men have quaint old-fashioned ways,
And every burn has ballad-lore,
  And every hamlet has its song,
And on its surf-beat rocky shore
  The eerie legend lingers long.
Old customs live there, unaware
  That they are garments cast away,
And what of light is shining there
  Is lingering light of yesterday.

Never to her the new day came,
  Or if it came she would not see;
This world of change was still the same
  To our old-world Penelope:
New fashions rose, old fashions went,
  But still she wore the same brocade,

With lace of Valenciennes or Ghent
　　More dainty by her darning made,
A little patch upon her face,
　　A tinge of colour on her cheek,
A frost of powder, just to grace
　　The locks that time began to streak.

A stately lady; to the poor
　　Her manner was without reproach;
But from the Causeway she was sure
　　To snub the Provost in his coach:
In pride of birth she did not seek
　　Her scorn of upstarts to conceal,
But of a Bailie's wife would speak
　　As if she bore the fisher's creel.
She said it képt them in their place,
　　Their fathers were of low degree;
She said the only saving grace
　　Of upstarts was humility.

The quaint, old Doric still she used,
　　And it came kindly from her tongue;
And oft the "mim-folk" she abused,
　　Who mincing English said or sung:
She took her claret, nothing loth,
　　Her snuff that one small nostril curled;

She might rap out a good round oath,
  But would not mince it for the world :
And yet the wild word sounded less
  In that Scotch tongue of other days ;
'Twas just like her old-fashioned dress,
  And part of her old-fashioned ways.

At every fair her face was known,
  Well-skilled in kyloes and in queys ;
And well she led the fiddler on
  To " wale " the best of his strathspeys ;
Lightly she held the man who rose
  While the toast-hammer still could rap,
And brought her gossip to a close,
  Or spoilt her after-dinner nap ;
Tea was for women, wine for men,
  And if they quarrelled o'er their cups,
They might go to the peat-moss then,
  And fight it out like stags or tups.

She loved a bishop or a dean,
  A surplice or a rocket well,
At all the Church's feasts was seen,
  And called the Kirk, Conventicle ;
Was civil to the minister,
  But stiff and frigid to his wife,

And looked askance, and sniffed at her,
　　As if she lived a dubious life.
But yet his sick her cellars knew,
　　Well stored from Portugal or France,
'And many a savoury soup and stew
　　Her game-bags furnished to the Manse.

But if there was a choicer boon
　　Above all else she would have missed,
It was on Sunday afternoon
　　To have her quiet game at whist
Close to the window, when the Whigs
　　Were gravely passing from the Kirk,
And some on foot, and some in gigs,
　　Would stare at her unhallowed work :
She gloried in her "devil's books"
　　That cut' their sour hearts to the quick;
Rather than miss their wrathful looks
　　She would have almost lost the trick.

Her politics were of the age
　　Of Claverhouse or Bolingbroke;
Still at the Dutchman she would rage,
　　And still of gallant Grahame she spoke.
She swore 'twas right that Whigs should die
　　Psalm-snivelling in the wind and rain,

Though she would ne'er have harmed a fly
　　For buzzing on the window pane.
And she had many a plaintive rhyme
　　Of noble Charlie and his men :
For her there was no later time,
　　All history had ended then.

The dear old sinner ! yet she had
　　A kindly human heart, I wot,
And many a sorrow she made glad,
　　And many a tender mercy wrought :
And though her way was somewhat odd,
　　Yet in her way she feared the Lord,
And thought she best could worship God
　　By holding Pharisees abhorred,
By being honest, fearless, true,
　　And thorough both in word and deed,
And by despising what is new,
　　And clinging to her old-world creed.

Wagstaff.

With supple form, and radiant face,
  And shock of swirling Auburn hair,
And brown plaid, worn with careless grace,
  He sauntered, loitering everywhere;
For his swift-glancing eye must look
  On all that met him by the way,
And every street was like a book
  Which he could read the live-long day:
Nor sun nor moon nor star nor chime
Set punctual tide for him or time,
For all his habits were at strife
With orderly mechanic life;
And in the Mart when he was seen,
Where sharp wits drove their bargains keen,
His wayward thoughts were oft astray,
  Brooding with Ruskin on St. Mark's,
Or dreaming on some broomy brae
  Among the linnets and the larks.

No flower that in the garden grows
  But all its way of life he knew,
No wilding in the green hedgerows
  But he could tell its story true ;
And where birds nestled, how they sung,
  And where to find the honey bees,
What varying notes were heard among
  The beech-woods and the stiff pine trees,
All sights and sounds of Nature, well
Their nicest difference he could tell ;
For where the careless footstep trod
He saw the glory and power of God.
All beauty thrilled him like the kiss
Of young love in its blushing bliss ;
And so his life had great delight,
  For beauty everywhere he met ;
A moss would make his eye grow bright,
  A cowslip or a violet.

The music of the ancient days,
  The pictures of the age of faith,
When Song was still the voice of Praise,
  And Worship had its vital breath
In forms of loveliness divine—
  Virgin and babe of tender grace—

He would be drunken as with wine
  On holy hymn or saintly face.
And O to hear him, when he met,
With some new loan, an ancient debt,
Come back to Keats's picture-words
Like flowers and fruits and singing birds,
Or Wordsworth's touch of Truth, who saw
All nature wrapt in love and awe.
Or Shelley's strains, like Lark unseen
  In mystic sweetness rippling on,
Or the choice words, and vision keen,
  And perfect art of Tennyson !

He had large wealth of curious lore,
  And freely would his wealth dispense,
And still his speech suggested more
  Than lay in its familiar sense;
And we who gathered round him, young
  And eager, inspiration caught
From broken fragments which he sung,
  Or glimpses of far-reaching thought.
In letters some, and some in Art,
And some in Science took their part;
But all ascribed to him that they
Had found their true life and its way :

Meanwhile he struggled lonely, poor,
Indebted, slighted, and obscure,
And went through darkness into rest;
  But yet his thoughts with us abide;
He lives in us, when we are best,
  He is but changed and multiplied.

Peppe.

Ugly was not the word for Peppe:
  His cheek was scarred with a crimson gash,
He had squinting eyes, and a limping step,
  And a long lip furzed with a red moustache,
Sharp-pointed teeth, like a saw, and black
  Finger-nails, like a vulture's claw,
And all the skin of him spotted and slack,
  Like a mouldy old parchment deed of the law.

Yet never maiden had silkier curls
  Scented and glossy and soft as a dove;
And never silkier voice among girls
  Lisped, in soft accents, of beauty and love;
Oiliest curls, and the oiliest speech
  Talking the wildest thoughts ever I heard—
Thoughts of a kind it were fitter to screech,
  Dropt like the notes of a sweet-singing bird.

Softly he spoke about fell Revolutions,
  Of Rank, Rule, and Title and Capital gone,

Swift overthrow of our old institutions,
  And blood from the Barricades splashing the
    throne,
Burning of churches, and burying gods,
  Treating the priests like the rats in their holes,
Ruin of all our old life with its modes
  Of building up order, and saving of souls.

Sometimes he went off, when little expected,
  But to come back, when as little desired,
Now looking haggard and lean and dejected,
  Tricked now in garb that he plainly admired;
Leaving, he went where no seeking could find him,
  Returning, no care could escape from his view,
And when he went, he left trouble behind him,
  And coming back, he brought trouble anew.

For, be his luck what it might, we were sure
  Storms would be brewing the moment he came,
Chills would be falling on friendships pure,
  Doubts would be cast upon some honoured name:
Mischief followed wherever he went,
  And some bright eyes would with tears be dim;
And yet he looked smiling and innocent,
  And we never could bring the thing home to
    him.

Last time we met was in seventy-two,
    Just when the mad Commune had burst;
Jewelled and furred like a Rotterdam Jew,
    Hardly I knew the fellow at first;
But he came up with a smile, and a look
    Nothing could ever the least embarrass,
Saying, Ah! here is your wished-for Book,
    And I picked it up at the siege of Paris.

Eh? was I wrong to give him his price,   .
    Instead of giving him straight in charge?
A book so scarce it was only twice
    Offered for sale to the world at large!
Ah! I so longed for it! just at the sight,
    I felt a knocking about my knee :—
And in the fury of that wild night,
    Strange that the rogue should have thought about
        me !

I knew that one in the Louvre lay :—
    O what a hang-dog look he had!
And something within me tried to say,
    "Now, if you buy it, you're just as bad."
Yet I must have it; there is a score
    Will give him his money if I refuse—
To think of me, now, in that wild uproar !
    And he saved it perhaps from the Petroleuse!

John Meff, M.A.

Alas ! he had outlived respect,
And the sharp sting of cold neglect,
And cared not wisely to reflect
    Upon his ways,
Or to look back, or to expect
    More happy days.

Once a rare scholar, ripe and full,
Famed Latinist in Classic School,
Whose biting satire scourged a fool
    With lash of scorn :
An Epigrammatist by rule,
    And native-born ;

Well could he tilt, and featly hit
Opponents with quotation fit
Of Attic or Horatian wit
    That made them wince,
Nor heeded if his weapon smit
    Or Priest or Prince.

Well could he, too, with mocking lip,
Sneer at the sciolists who slip
On niceties of scholarship,
         Nor would abate
The lash of that contemptuous whip
         For love or hate.

So wrath had gathered round his life,
And love had fallen away, and strife
Had grown its crop of quarrels rife
         Until he stood,
Having nor lover, friend, nor wife,
         In solitude.

Then nights and suppers, deemed divine
Symposia of Falernian wine,
And Syren songs that turn to swine
         Who list to hear,
To these he greatly did incline
         Both heart and ear :

At first with shame ; but soon he fell
A willing captive to their spell,
And grew a taproom Oracle
         To yokels fuddled,
Or mad with fiery drink, or well
         With beer bemuddled.

Now far from him Professor's chair,
And High School with its classic air,
And to the Kirk he may not dare
  Lift up his hopes ;
For he is bound to shame and care
  By devil's ropes.

Yet far away in moorland cot
Where first he tasted life's hard lot,
His early promise, ne'er forgot,
  Has ne'er grown dim,
And there is still a bright green spot
  On earth for him.

All else forgetting—pride of fame,
A happy home, an honoured name,
And God and truth, and praise and blame,
  He will not let
His frail old mother know the shame
  Of want or debt.

She wots not how his days are spent,
But fails not of her yearly rent,
Nor homely fare, nor clothing sent
  From him threadbare,
Nor weekly letter kindly meant
  To ease her care.

o

And still she tells of him with pride,
How with the minister he vied
In learning, and had never lied
  As boy or man,
Nor from his mother aught would hide
  Since life began.

A dutiful and loving son !
A scholar who great fame had won !
She other wish on earth had none
  Except to reach
Some place, before her race was run,
  To hear him preach !

O mystic shuttles, how ye dart
Through life's dim web ! O thou that art
Still clinging to a better part
  Mid all thy wrong !
And O the pathos of the heart,
  Believing long !

Tatto.

A deep, grey eye, a meek, grey face,
  Grey sandy hair, and garb worn grey,
A limp loose form, a hurried pace
  That loitered never by the way,
  And knew no leisure and no play,
A wistful look of painëd thought,
  As if he must, yet feared to think,
For his too daring Reason wrought
  Dread of itself, as on the brink
  Of chasms from which he fain would shrink:
Much-pondering, his soul could see
But God in all the things that be,
In subtle matter, and changeful force,
In joy and anguish and remorse;
No dual empire could he find,
But all was matter, and all was mind.
So had he lost his early faiths,
  And glory of his simple youth,
And this had been like many deaths,
  Though dying into larger truth.

This world, he said, all things divine
  Are but the great God's uttered thought:
His work is not like thine or mine
  Which brains have planned, and tools have wrought;
  It is, yet out of Him, is not.
He makes the light, He makes the shade
  That limits it with form; yet light
Is nothing but the ripple made
  By rhythmic motion, giving sight
  And wondrous vision of delight.
And shadow too is nothing. Why,
My shadow surely is not I;
'Tis nothing; yet I make it; well
My form and features it shall tell,
And yet I use no art to make
This nothing, which for me you take.—
Thus dreamily the mystic spoke,
  And ever as his thought was spent,
It rose again like wave that broke
  In never-ending argument.

For all his thoughts of soul and mind
  Were shaped by hard material law;
And yet no matter could he find,
  But mind created what it saw,
  And of its shadows stood in awe:

And God was all. The solid earth,
  The rivers and the shining seas,
And all to which the heavens gave birth,
  And all the rocks and hills and trees,
  And grass and flowers and birds and bees,
All were but pictured thoughts which shone
As sparks from rapid wheel are thrown,
And gleam out in the dark, and then
Pass into nothingness again.
Yet while the world he thus refined
Into fine forms of subtle mind,
The subtle mind he made again
  Gross by material forms of thought,
And chemic forces in the brain
  Our vices and our virtues wrought.

Still gathering knowledge, day by day,
  Unwearying in his search for light,
He gathered scruples by the way,
  Till scarce one way of life seemed right,
  And he was in a helpless plight.
He scrupled at the Church's creed,
  Although he held her mission grand;
He scrupled at all paths which lead
  To honour in an ancient land
  Whose bridges have the ages spanned:

He scrupled at the tricks and lies,
Unscrupulous, of merchandise;
And while all science he pursued
He held no art or practice good,
Till, as by threads of cob-web dim,
All paths of life seemed shut to him;
For still the scrupulous conscience stood
   And barred the way when it should lead,
And made him helpless unto good,
   That he from evil might be freed.

Fain would we laugh his scruples down,
   But there his truth rebuked our mirth;
He sought not riches or renown,
   Nor any fatness of the earth,
   Might he but keep his honest worth;
No envy had he of the great,
   No drop of bitterness had he,
He was contented with the state
   Of noble-minded poverty,
   Well-pleased of no account to be.
To hammer great thoughts out of stones,
And fossil leaves, and scales and bones;
To give imagination wings,
And frame the universe of things
From chaos, or from nothing—that

Was all he cared to labour at.
And so he drifted still along,
    Having no social roots or ties,
Self-fettered by his scruples strong,
    Yet making many good and wise.

Mother-in-Law.

O my boy ! O my heart it will break !
  And how like his father he sat !
So cruel and cold ! and his voice did not shake,
When he shattered my life and my hope for the sake
  Of a creature like that !

Not that it matters how soon
  My poor dregs of life may depart :
What are we mothers made for, but to croon
A soft cradle-song to a low cradle-tune
  With a slow-breaking heart ?

O Woman ! whose love is thy life,
  Thy love-life is sorrow and pain ;
As the girl's love dawns, so her troubles grow rife,
And they darken on down through the mother and
      wife,
  Drip-dripping like rain.

O my boy ! and I hoped, when they brought
  My baby to lie on my breast,
Now, at length, I shall find all the love I have sought,
Now, at length, I shall bask in the bliss I have got,
  And my heart shall have rest.

From me thy life came, and by me
  Shall its young powers be nourished alone ;
No wanton shall poison its pure springs to thee
With milk of coarse passion, but it shall all be
  Sweet and clean as my own.

And so, with pained pleasure, he drew
  His life, day by day, out of mine,
And mine was the one tender hand that he knew :
I suffered none else, for his kiss was like dew,
  And his breath like warm wine.

O my beauty ! my hero ! What dreams
  I dreamed, as he smiled in my face !
What hopes lit my life as with laughing sun-gleams,
When I kissed into silence his lustiest screams
  With a mirthful embrace.

Now, I pictured him soldier of fame
  Battling on in the thick of the fight ;

Now, a statesman whose eloquence kindled a flame
That fired all the land, till they shouted his name
   As the symbol of right.

Then I sighed, and said, Let him be good,
   And I heed not what else is in store :
But ah ! that was not what the mother's heart would,
And still it went back to its loftier mood,
   And panted for more.

And what, if God, wroth at my pride,
   Has humbled me now for my sin ?
For I knew in my heart, when I said it, I lied ;
And I knew it was dull moral prosing to hide
   The proud thought within.

I gave up all, all for my boy—
   All the world where, they said, I once shone ;
And the girl-wife, tremulous, timid and coy,
Grew strong in the pride of a mother's great joy,
   And for him lived alone.

I grudged every moment away,
   I grudged every task not for him ;
As he lay on my lap, I would croodle and play,
As he lay in soft sleep, I would watch him and pray
   Till my wet eyes grew dim.

I grudged even his father, when he
  Would toss up my child in the air,
Or when he would ride the high-horse on his knee,
Or the little one laughed aloud in his glee,
  As he tangled his hair.

But sometimes, I thought, it were good
  That another should come to divide
This so jealous love with its passionate mood ;
Yet what other baby, like him, ever could
  Be my joy and pride ?

Then I'd clasp him close to my breast,
  And kiss him, body and limb ;
It was wicked to dream even, or say it in jest,
That another could ever be fondly caressed
  With the love I gave him.

And then as he grew up apace,
  I went back to schooling once more,
And took up old studies of number and case,
And the great tale of Troy, and of that haughty race
  By the brown Tiber's shore.

For I trembled to think he might read
  What from youth should be hidden with care,

And be smirched with some grossness of word or deed,
Or filled with false thoughts, that like thistle-down seed
   Fly about in the air.

O my boy ! O the bliss of those days,
   When I pored o'er his Latin and Greek !
And I knew all his thoughts, and I saw all his plays,
And I noted him manly and bright in his ways,
   And gentle and meek.

And now comes this woman to steal
   All the fruit of my life and its bliss,
All the joy and the hope that I ever shall feel,
And plants me a· death-wound nothing can heal
   With her Judas-like kiss.

She is years and years older than he,
   And has trapped him, I know, with her guile,
For there's nothing he'll hear now, and nothing will
     see
But goodness in her, and unfairness in me,
   As he basks in her smile.

Poor boy ! if you knew ! That wan smile
   Has been tried upon scores before you ;
'Tis a well-worn look, you might see, by its style,

Has done duty for years, for her eyes, the meanwhile
  Are not smiling nor true.

Charm ! ay, such as practised ones wield ;
  With a hard, hungry look in her eye,
And a lithe, supple form, and a heart that is steeled,
Which no love can touch, and which no love will yield,
  Till the day that she die.

Of course he must marry her now ;
  He has gone quite too far to draw back ;
But O what a sorrow is hid in the vow
To love the unloving, and make his heart bow
  To the yoke till it crack !

She has poisoned his mind against me,
  And will poison it more if she can :
O that poor jealous heart of hers ! Can he not see,
It is not like a mother's ? But no one can be
  Half so blind as a man.

No ; their wedding I will not go near ;
  I never will darken her door,
Nor break bread of her's, nor partake of her cheer —
Far rather I'd follow my boy on his bier
  To his rest evermore !

I have thought, if I only could see
   A baby of his in my lap,
A baby of his smiling up from my knee,
·O to nurse both mother and baby would be
   The blessedest hap !

But she ! that woman ! her child !
   Do you wonder it makes me sad,
When I know that my boy has been so beguiled ?
It is weeks and months since ever I've smiled,
   And it's making me bad.

She is deep—O she well knows her game !—
   And is ever so gentle and meek ;
She sees I don't like her ; but loves all the same
Every one that he loves, every one of his name,
   All the days of the week !

And that drives me mad, for I know
   He believes every word that she says.
If only by word or by look she would shew
The false, scheming heart that is hidden below
   Her soft, silky ways !

And her cunning is breeding hate,
   And wickedest thoughts in me :

She might be another man's happy mate,
But to me and my house she is like a Fate
  That I shudder to see.

God, keep me from sin and wrath :
  Had I lived in the old Greek time,—
Hate killed the King of men in his bath ;
And I might have sown too the aftermath
  Of a horrible crime ?

Who knows what one might have been ?
  Who knows what the heart might do ?
O the thoughts of guilt I have sometimes seen,
Trying the shape of their guilt to screen
  From my doubtful view !

And my husband goes, meanwhile,
  Careless and easy of heart,
Daffing my cares with a mocking smile ;
Ay, that was ever his hateful style
  Of playing his part.

And my boy grows like him in that,
  Liker him every day ;
And O so cruel and cool as he sat !
And O so lightly he jested at
  What I tried to say.

Once how I hoped he would wed—
  For I know that she loves him dear—
That saintly child of the sainted dead !
They were born for each other, I always said,
  The self-same year.

But my wishes are nothing to him :
  I am blind, of course, as a bat,
For my eyes with the tears of love are dim ;
And my cup of sorrow is filled to the brim
  For a creature like that.

O mothers ! whose love is such bliss
  While the baby lies soft on your knee,
With each fond word, and each rapturous kiss,
Ye are sowing the seeds of a grief like this
  Which has come to me.

Father-in-Law.

Never mind what your mother may say :
  She was always hard on the girls :
Your virtuous women have all a way
Of saying the bitterest things they may
  About them and their curls.

It is different, now, with a man :
  The better he is, I think,
He'll speak of young fellows the best that he can,
Though the rogues may be learning to curse and ban,
  And play, too, and drink.

Well ; that never struck me until
  I said it, and yet it is true ;
Good men could not do what your good women will,
And they call it a duty they have to fulfil
  In pure love to you.

I am not good, myself, as you know,
  And I never pretended to be ;

P

And I've sometimes thought I was happier so
Than to purse up my mouth, and look glum as I go
   At the things that I see.

But your mother is virtuous, lad;
   Whatever she is, she is that;
A virtuous woman, for good or bad,
And she's fretting her soul, till it's really sad,
   At this wooing you're at.

She won't let me rest till I speak
   My mind on't, and here's what I say:
Maybe her reasons are poor and weak,
And she's hot and hysteric, and not very meek;
   But she'll have her own way.

Don't insist upon your way, at least;
   It was always my plan to give in,
And to make as if I would do as she pleased,
Till she cooled down a bit; for her keenness ceased
   As she thought she would win.

Well; I know that she always meant
   You, some day or other, should wed
That putty-faced doll of a baby-saint,
With her breath smelling ever so sickly and faint,
   As if more than half-dead.

I am glad you are out of that mess;
   It would never have turned out well:
She has not the breeding, the mouth, or the pace,
And what your mother can see in her face
   I never could tell.

And it's right you should choose your own wife;
   I did it, and every man should;
It is hard that another should tie you for life,
Maybe to bother, vexation, and strife:
   Though she means it for good.

But you'd better give up your first 'flame,'
   Nearly every man does that I know;
Your mother is wild when I name but her name,
And it would not be nice for a girl if she came
   To be ill-treated so.

I allow she is quiet and good,
   And handsome and ladylike too,
She can ride too, and talk and dress as she should,
And she is not at all of hysterical mood,
   And you say she loves you.

But your mother can't bear her, you see;
   That don't go for much, I admit,

Our mothers are fain we should always be
Still the small babies that sat on their knee,
  Admiring their wit.

But I am told she is older than you;
  Of course, that's a matter of taste,
And old or young, they will always do
Just what they like; yet it's also true
  You should not be in haste.

If she had but a trifle of cash!
  I don't mind the two or three years;
They're not here or there; but it's something rash
To dive into wedlock, you see, with a splash,
  When, for aught that appears,

You have not between you, I think,
  Enough to pay for your tour;
And how you're to live, and to eat and drink,
Is more than I know; but it's all rose-pink
  To-day, to be sure.

Now, I have not a shilling to spare,
  Not a penny to play pitch and toss;
And you'd not like your mother to sit down with care
Before she is Dowager, and you are heir
  Of the peat-hag and moss.

You must not count, then, on me :
  I never could keep out of debt ;
But I'll leave you a name, and a family tree
Long held in honour, and bills two or three
  That are not honoured yet.

There's the old coach I had to renew,
  The horses not fit for the road,
And the cellar quite empty ; and what could I do ?
For the rents were all spent ere a guinea was due,
  When I last went abroad.

You'd not wish to see me drive out
  With a chaise, and a pair of old screws,
And bring from the grocer's a bottle of stout ;
No, there's things one must have, and yet cannot
    without
  The help of the Jews.

But one should be able to do
  Without luxuries, now, like books,
And pictures and china and ormolu,
And a wife that will always want something new,
  For her handsome looks.

Have you thought at all how you're to live,
  With taxes to pay, and your rent ?
You may run into debt, and your tradesmen grieve ;

With your name, you may borrow, although you must
    give
  A heavy per cent.

But it's ticklish work doing that long,
  And you can't trust the cards or the dice,
And betting without ready money is wrong;
And what can you do that is worth an old song,
  When you've tried it twice?

A Lawyer that has but one brief,
  A Doctor one patient who tends,
May marry, in hope that on turning the leaf,
By healing a fool, or releasing a thief,
  He may make what he spends.

But there's no kind of work now for you,
  And nothing to hope that I see,
Unless I should die for fond lovers and true,
Which is hard for a man in his sixties to do,
  With but gout in his knee.

You must think of it better; and mind,
  Not a word to your mother that's rough:
She is hot and hysterical, maybe, and blind,
But then she's your mother, and ever was kind;
  And that is enough.

Daughter-in-Law.

So, there; you have told me all;
  And you want to know what we must do;
Your love is great, but your purse is small,
And you leave me free, if I like, to fall
  From my word to you.

But what, if I am not free
  To take my freedom again?
What, if this foolish heart in me
Rather far would be bound than be
  Without its chain?

It is not the promise that binds,
  But the love that changeth not;
And pledges taken of faithless minds
I hold them but as the idle winds
  Heard, and forgot.

I am bound, be your lot what it may,
  Bound fast, for I would not be free,

Bound by the love that will have its own way,
And will hold me for ever, whatever you say,
  And whatever you be.

Would you be richer without
  The love I have given to you?
Would you be abler to go about,
Doing your work without fear or doubt,
  Were I less true?

Ah! well; it might break my heart,
  But yet I could let it break,
If I thought you would play a nobler part,
While I pined away with this love-sick dart,
  And its life-long ache.

You would not? Your life would be wrecked?
  Nay, I dare not say that: yet I fear
It would not be good for your soul to reflect,
How the bloom and the glory of love had been checked
  In the spring o' the year.

It is bad, having once known the right,
  And the impulse of nobleness prized,
To accept the less worthy, and order the fight
For a cause that is meaner, and walk by a light
  That you once had despised.

I am not afraid to be poor,
　I am not afraid of toil,
With you I could labour, with you too endure;
But I fear to lose that keeps the flame of life pure
　As with sacred oil.

But we must not hurry or fret,
　Or think of ourselves alone;
Love waits for love, though the sun be set,
And the stars come out, and the dews are wet,
　And the night winds moan.

That which is thine must be mine—
　Home and friends and affairs,
Father and mother—mine and thine;
I have thy love, but I long and pine
　To have also theirs.

Your mother dislikes me, I see;
　Her face is hard and set
The moment she enters a room with me;
But if love will do it, I mean that she
　Shall love me yet.

Be still, and wait for the light;
　It is hard for a mother to part

With the son who made her life full and bright,
And to think that another woman has right
　　To his whole true heart.

I know what you must be to her,
　　For I know what you are now to me ;
I can feel how her bosom must throb and stir,
As if some robber of love I were
　　With a master-key.

But I will not part her and you :
　　I could not enter a home
To sever old ties so tender and true ;
Yea, let me rather bring fresh and new
　　For the days to come.

Ah me ! we are often unkind,
　　We who live for our love alone :
We think of ourselves, and are cold and blind
To the anxious heart, and the troubled mind
　　Half-turned to stone.

Like the dew in the heart of the flower
　　That bends with its burden of bliss,
Folding it close in the petalled bower,
You have lain in her heart from the first mother-hour
　　And the first mother-kiss.

And now from that heart's warm core
  Shall I drain off its fond-clasped joy?
Nay, but you shall be only her gladness more
Than all that you ever have been before
  As a man or boy.

Do you know that I like her the best?
  Your father is nice and free,
With his pleasant talk and his lightsome jest,
But he speaks and smiles unto all the rest
  As he does to me:

While she has a freezing look
  Whenever I come her way,
And the formal speech of a printed book,
Though I see with a friend in a quiet nook
  She is bright and gay.

But I know 'tis her love of you
  That makes her distrust me so;
And I like her for that, for I love you too,
And I think that her love of me will be as true,
  When she comes to know.

Daughter to her I will be,
  Love me she shall in the end;

Thoughtful and dutiful, you shall see
My love will find out the way, and she
   Shall call me a friend.

Let her be cross for a while,
   I will only be sweeter for that;
Let her frown if she will, I will meekly smile,
And let her scold, I will walk a mile
   To be rated at.

But love me she shall, if her heart
   Is as true as I think it to be;
Be patient, and see how I play my part,
And O my love will have perfect art,
   When I think of thee!

A Minister's Dilemma.

"Does any one forbid the banns?"
  I asked; and something in me cried,
And cried: Yea, I forbid this man's
  Unloving claim to loveless bride.
She is my friend's; he loved her well,
  And they were plighted years ago,
And still their coming marriage bell
  Rings hope into his heart, I know.
I cannot join this alien pair,
I cannot say the wedding prayer;
I cannot lie; nor God nor man
Could ever make them truly one:
Her face is pale, her hand is cold,
Not love has brought her here, but gold.—
I paused; and all was still as death;
  I looked around, but where was he?
I watched the quick heave of her breath;
  She dare not lift her eye to me.

'Twas all a lie—the solemn vow,
  The orange-blossom and the veil,
And wedding ring ; the prayer, I trow,
  Came from me sobbing, like a wail
For broken faith that breaketh hearts ;
  There was no blessing in its words,
There was no oneness in its parts,
  It was a jar of broken chords.

The Rival Brothers.

There were two brothers loved a maid,
    Well-a-day !
Side by side they had grown and played,
Yet were not liker than sun and shade :
    And the woods are green in May.

One was lord of the house and lands,
    Well-a-day !
From the heather hill to the rippled sands,
But the other he had the brains and hands ;
    And the woods are green in May.

One was sullen and hard and proud,
    Well-a-day !
The other he mixed with the common crowd,
Blythe as the lark that singeth loud,
    When the woods are green in May.

O a maiden's love must be wooed with care,
    Well-a-day !

It flits like the peewit here and there,
Hard to follow, and swift to scare;
   And the woods are green in May.

A maiden's love has its dainty wiles,
   Well-a-day!
Its glances coy, and its mocking smiles,
And is fain to linger by lanes and stiles,
   When the woods are green in May.

The laird he came with a high demand,
   Well-a-day!
And mickle he spake of his house and land,
And the braes that sloped to the bonnie sand,
   And the woods so green in May.

Lightly she laughed at the laird that morn,
   Well-a-day!
When I sell my love, she said with scorn,
It shall be for more than cows and corn;
   And the woods are green in May.

When I sell my love the price I set
   Well-a-day!
It will be an earl's fair coronet,
But it is not going to market yet;
   And the woods are green in May.

Ah ! Fate is subtle and deep and dark,
       Well-a-day !
'Tis not on the ship that he sets his mark,   '
But on the tree that shall wreck the barque,
    When the woods are green in May.

And grimly he watches the rotten wood,
       Well-a-day !
Builded in with the timbers good,
For the ship is laden with widowhood,
    And the woods are green in May.

O the rotten plank in her life was laid,
       Well-a-day !
That day when the light heart gaily said
His cows and corn might not buy a maid,
    And the woods are green in May.

Merrily by the trysting tree,
       Well-a-day !
She told the tale, and they laughed with glee
That night, the winsome brother and she,
    When the woods were green in May.

They went to the Kirk in the summer tide,
       Well-a-day !
       Q

A gallant lover and graceful bride,
Walking together side by side,
　　　O the woods are green in May.

They went to the Kirk and vowed the vow,
　　　Well-a-day !
And none was there but the priest, I trow,
And the blackbird singing upon the bough,
　　　And the woods are green in May.

O love is sweet with its trust complete,
　　　Well-a-day !
And the rains may fall, and the sun may beat,
But it cares not either for cold or heat;
　　　And the woods are green in May.

He had the brains, and he had the hands,
　　　Well-a-day !
But he was not lord of the house and lands,
And the bonnie green braes by the yellow sands,
　　　And the woods are green in May.

To London town their steps were bent,
　　　˙Well-a-day !
To the weary London streets they went,
And all but their wealth of love was spent
　　　Ere the woods were green in May.

He would coin his thoughts into heaps of gold,
       Well-a-day !
For his hope was high, and his heart was bold :
How oft is the tragic story told !
       And the woods are green in May.

Years came and went, and youths were men,
       Well-a-day !
They were ageing now who were stalwart then,
And the laird like an old bear kept his den,
       Though the woods were green in May.

Grim as a bear in his chimney nook,
       Well-a-day !
With a curse on his lip, and a frown in his look,
And a pipe and a mug and a great clasped book ;
       And the woods are green in May.

A widow came with her little child,
       Well-a-day !
And O but her face it was meek and mild !
And white as the daisy undefiled
       When the woods are green in May.

With a woful heart that was like to break,
       Well-a-day !

She prayed him, when she died, to take
Her little boy, for his father's sake;
  And the woods are green in May.

Might she but keep him for a space,
   Well-a-day!
Till heaven should take her in its grace
Again to look on her dear lord's face;
  And the woods are green in May.

Or if, alas! that might not be,
   Well-a-day!
She would be content her boy to see
Now and then by the trysting tree,
  Where the woods were green in May.

It's O so wily he smiled, and grim,
   Well-a-day!
The while she pleaded so meek with him,
And her eyes with the great salt tears grew dim
  And the woods are green in May.

Wily and hard, as he thought of that,
   Well-a-day!
He had been cunningly plotting at;
"So that," he said, "is your bastard brat;"
  And the woods are green in May.

" "Twas an ill market, I'll be sworn,
   Well-a-day !
When you sold your love for a wanton's scorn,
Which you would not sell for my cows and corn ; "
   And the woods are green in May.

O pale as death was her lily-white cheek,
   Well-a-day !
And then it flushed with a crimson streak,
And the flash of her eye was no longer meek ;
   And the woods are green in May.

And the glance of her scorn he ill could brook,
   Well-a-day !
Crouching there in the chimney nook
With his pipe and his mug and his great clasped book;
   O the woods are green in May !

She turned her right and round about,
   Well-a-day !
She could not breathe for a fearful doubt,
Yet O so stately as she went out,
   And the woods are green in May.

Stately and grand she turned from him.
   Well-a-day !

But her head was dizzy, her eyes were dim,
As she dragged her steps through the meadows trim;
  O the woods are green in May !

The steers were slumbering in the shade,
   Well-a-day !
And she saw the deer in the leafy glade
'Mong the tall green fern and the foxglove wade ;
  And the woods are green in May.

But straight to the ivied Kirk she went,
   Well-a-day !
And her thin hand shook, and her heart grew faint
As over the great paged book she bent ;
  And the woods are green in May.

For wedding record there was none,
   Well-a-day !
And the grey old priest was dead and gone,
And she was a widow and all alone :
  And the woods are green in May.

" O mother, your hand it is cold as stone,
   Well-a-day !
O mother, your grip it will crush my bone,
But I would not heed if you would not moan ; "
  And the woods are green in May.

" He did not mean it—he could not know,"
Well-a-day !
She groaned, and her voice was hollow and low,
And her face was set with a death-like woe :
O the woods are green in May.

" My boy, your father loved us well,
Well-a-day !
You never must dream he had that to tell
Which might have sunk a soul to hell."
O the woods are green in May.

She led him out by the low Kirk-door,
Well-a-day !
She led him down to the yellow shore,
And they were not heard of evermore.
But the woods were green in May.

END.

PRINTED BY ROBERT MACLEHOSE, GLASGOW.

WORKS PUBLISHED BY
MR. MACLEHOSE,

Publisher to the University of Glasgow.

SAINT VINCENT STREET, GLASGOW.

Published by
JAMES MACLEHOSE, GLASGOW,
Publisher to the University.

LONDON: MACMILLAN AND CO.

London,	.	.	.	*Hamilton, Adams & Co.*
Cambridge,	.	.	.	*Macmillan & Co.*
Edinburgh,	.		.	*Douglas & Foulis.*
Dublin,			.	*W. H. Smith & Son.*

MDCCCLXXXI.

MR. MACLEHOSE'S
Catalogue of Books.

ARGYLL, Duke of—WHAT THE TURKS ARE; AND HOW WE HAVE BEEN HELPING THEM. Speech delivered in the City Hall, Glasgow, September 19, 1876. By His Grace the DUKE OF ARGYLL, K.T. With a Preface. Second Edition. 8vo. 1s.

ARGYLL, Duke of—SPEECH ON THE CONDUCT OF THE FOREIGN OFFICE DURING THE INSURRECTION IN CRETE IN 1867. 8vo. 6d.

ANDERSON—CLINICAL LECTURES ON THE CURABILITY OF ATTACKS OF TUBERCULAR PERITONITIS AND ACUTE PHTHISIS (GALLOPING CONSUMPTION). By T. M'CALL ANDERSON, M.D., Professor of Clinical Medicine in the University of Glasgow. Crown 8vo, Illustrated with Wood Engravings. 2s. 6d.

ANDREWS—THE PSYCHOLOGY OF SCEPTICISM AND PHENO-MENALISM. By JAMES ANDREWS. Crown 8vo. 2s. 6d.

BANNATYNE—GUIDE TO THE REGIMENTAL EXAMINATION FOR PROMOTION OF OFFICERS IN THE INFANTRY. Part I. —Containing what is required by Her Majesty's Regulations to qualify for promotion to the Rank of LIEU-TENANT. By LIEUTENANT COLONEL BANNATYNE. Sixteenth Edition, carefully revised. 1880. Small 8vo. 7s.

BANNATYNE—GUIDE TO THE REGIMENTAL EXAMINATION FOR PROMOTION OF OFFICERS IN THE INFANTRY. Part II. Containing what is required by Her Majesty's Regulations, in addition to the subjects comprised in Part I., to qualify for Promotion to the Rank of CAPTAIN. Thirteenth Edition, carefully revised. 1880. Small 8vo. 7s. [*In preparation.*

BANNATYNE — INSTRUCTIONS FOR THE PAYMENT OF TROOPS AND COMPANIES IN THE CAVALRY AND INFANTRY, founded on the Queen's and War Office Regulations. Small 8vo. New and greatly enlarged Edition. 6s.

BANNATYNE—BRIGADE DRILL, in the form of Question and Answer, founded on the Field Exercise and Evolutions of Infantry. Small 8vo. 1s.

BATHGATE—COLONIAL EXPERIENCES; OR SKETCHES OF PEOPLE AND PLACES IN THE PROVINCE OF OTAGO, NEW ZEALAND. By A. BATHGATE, Dunedin. Crown 8vo. 7s. 6d.

"Anybody who may be desirous of getting an idea of the real state of matters in New Zealand, cannot do better than read Mr. Bathgate's pleasant, chatty, unpretending colonial experiences."—*Leeds Mercury.*

BLACKBURN—THE PIPITS. By the Author of "Caw, Caw," with Sixteen page Illustrations by J. B. (MRS. HUGH BLACKBURN). 4to. 3s.

"This is a charming fable in verse, illustrated by the well-known J. B., whose power in delineating animals, especially birds, is scarcely inferior to Landseer or Rosa Bonheur."—*Courant.*

BORLAND HALL, by the Author of "OLRIG GRANGE." *See* SMITH.

BROWN—The Life of a Scottish Probationer. Being the Memoir of Thomas Davidson, with his Poems and Letters. By the Rev. James Brown, D.D., Minister of St. James' Church, Paisley. Second Edition. With Portrait. Crown 8vo. 7s. 6d.

" A charming little biography. His was one of those rare natures which fascinates all who come in contact with it."—*Spectator.*

" It is an unspeakable pleasure to a reviewer weary of wading through piles of commonplace to come unexpectedly on a prize such as this."—*Nonconformist.*

" A very fresh and interesting little book."—*Saturday Review.*

BUCHANAN—Camp Life in the Crimea as Seen by a Civilian. A Personal Narrative by George Buchanan, M.A., M.D., Professor of Clinical Surgery in the University of Glasgow. Crown 8vo. 7s. 6d.

BUCHANAN—Inaugural Address. Delivered in the University of Glasgow. By Professor Buchanan. 8vo. 1s.

CAIRD, Principal—An Introduction to the Philosophy of Religion. By the Very Reverend John Caird, D.D., Principal and Vice-Chancellor of the University of Glasgow, and one of Her Majesty's Chaplains for Scotland. Demy 8vo. 10s. 6d.

" It is the business of the reviewer to give some notion of the book which he reviews, either by a condensation of its contents or by collecting the cream in the shape of short selected passages ; but this cannot be done with a book like the one before us, of which the argument does not admit of condensation, and which is all cream.........The most valuable book of its kind that has appeared."—Mr. T. H. Green in *The Academy.*

" It is remarkable also for its marvellous power of exposition and graceful subtlety of thought. Hegel's solution of the problem of religion is at length adequately represented in English literature. Hegelianism has never appeared so attractive as it appears in the clear and fluent pages of Principal Caird."—*Spectator.*

" This is in many respects a remarkable book, and perhaps the most important contribution to the subject with which it deals that has been made in recent years."—*Mind*, October 1880.

" To many a student the reading of this book will mark an intellectual and spiritual epoch."— *The Nation* (New York).

CAIRD, Principal—UNIVERSITY SERMONS AND LECTURES. 8vo. 1s. each.

1. WHAT IS RELIGION? A Sermon preached before the University, at the Opening of the University Chapel. 1871.
2. CHRISTIAN MANLINESS. A Sermon preached before the University, at the Opening of the Winter Session, 1871.
3. IN MEMORIAM. A Sermon preached before the University on occasion of the Death of the Very REV. THOMAS BARCLAY, D.D., Principal of the University.
4. THE UNIVERSAL RELIGION. A Lecture delivered in Westminster Abbey, on the day of Intercession for Missions.
5. THE UNITY OF THE SCIENCES. A Lecture delivered at the Opening of the Winter Session. 1874.
6. THE PROGRESSIVENESS OF THE SCIENCES. A Lecture delivered at the Opening of the Winter Session. 1875.

CAIRD, Professor E.—A CRITICAL ACCOUNT OF THE PHILOSOPHY OF KANT : with an Historical Introduction. By EDWARD CAIRD, M.A., LL.D., Professor of Moral Philosophy in the University of Glasgow, and late Fellow and Tutor of Merton College, Oxford. 8vo. 18s.

"This book contains the most exhaustive and most valuable exposition of Kant's metaphysical system which has appeared in this country. The critical analysis is incisive and searching, and the exposition plain and unambiguous. The running commentary is the work of a man who both knows what he has to say, and knows how to say it forcibly and well. The style is attractive as well as clear. Without being ornate or rhetorical, it has about it a kind of quiet eloquence which comes of conscious strength and of genuine conviction."—*The Times.*

"Mr. Caird's statement of the Kantian doctrine is singularly felicitous. The simplification is at once full, accurate, and unbiased."—MR. T. H. GREEN in the *Academy.*

"No account of Kant's Philosophy has ever appeared in England so full, so intelligible, and so interesting to read as this work by Professor Caird. It is *the* English Book on Kant."—*Contemporary Review.*

CAMERON—LIGHT, SHADE, AND TOIL : POEMS. By WILLIAM C. CAMERON, Shoemaker. With Introductory Note by the REV. WALTER C. SMITH, D.D. Extra fcap. 8vo. 6s.

CLELAND—Evolution, Expression, and Sensation, by John Cleland, M.D., F.R.S., Professor of Anatomy in the University of Glasgow. Crown 8vo. [*In the Press.*

DAVIDSON—Life of—*See* Brown's Life of Davidson.

DEAS—History of the Clyde to the Present Time. With Maps and Diagrams. New Edition Enlarged. By James Deas, M. Inst. C.E., Engineer of the Clyde Navigation. 8vo. 10s. 6d.

" Mr. Deas tells his story in a very clear and concise way."—*Saturday Review.*

DERBY, Earl of—Inaugural Address, delivered to the University of Glasgow, on his Installation as Lord Rector of the University. By the Right Honourable The Earl of Derby. 8vo. 1s.

DICKSON—Pleading in the Courts of Law of Scotland. An Address delivered before the Glasgow Juridical Society. By W. Gillespie Dickson, LL.D., Advocate, late Sheriff of Lanarkshire. 8vo. 1s.

DICKSON—Introductory Lecture. Delivered at the Opening of the Divinity Hall, in the University of Glasgow, Session 1873-74. By William Purdie Dickson, D.D., Professor of Divinity. 8vo. 1s.

DODS—On Preaching, an Address delivered to the Students of the Free Church College, Glasgow, by Marcus Dods, D.D. Second Edition, 8vo. 6d.

DOTTY and other Poems by J. L. Extra Fcap. 8vo. 3s. 6d.

EGGS 4D. A DOZEN, AND CHICKENS 4D. A POUND
ALL THE YEAR ROUND. Containing full and com-
plete information for successful and profitable keeping of
Poultry. Small 8vo. Cheap Edition in Paper Covers.
Seventeenth Thousand. 1s.

"No book has appeared for many years that discusses the subject so
explicitly and exhaustively."—*Daily Review.*

EWING—MEMOIR OF JAMES EWING, ESQ., of Strathleven.
Formerly Lord Provost of Glasgow, and M.P. for that City.
By the late REV. MACINTOSH MACKAY, LL.D. Fcap. 4to.
With Portrait. 21s.

GAIRDNER—FLUCTUATIONS IN TRADE. A Lecture delivered
to the Institute of Accountants. By CHARLES GAIRDNER,
Manager of the Union Bank of Scotland. Third Edition.
Demy 8vo. 1s.

GAIRDNER, Professor—TWO LECTURES ON BOOKS AND
PRACTICAL TEACHING, AND ON CLINICAL INSTRUCTION.
Being Introductory Addresses delivered in the University
of Glasgow, and in the Western Infirmary. By W. T.
GAIRDNER, M.D., Professor of Practice of Medicine in the
University of Glasgow, Physician in Ordinary to Her
Majesty the Queen in Scotland. 8vo. 1s.

GEMMEL—THE TIBERIAD ; or, The Art of Hebrew Accen-
tuation. A Didactive Poem, in Three Books. By JOHN
GEMMEL, M.A., Senior Minister of Free Church at Fairlie.
Extra fcap. 8vo. 3s.

GLASGOW—THE OLD COUNTRY HOUSES OF THE OLD
GLASGOW GENTRY. Illustrated by permanent Photographs.
Royal 4to. Half Red Morocco. Gilt Top. Second Edition.
Very scarce. £10, 10s.

This is a history of one hundred of the old houses in and around
Glasgow, and of the families who owned and lived in them. To the
local antiquary it is especially interesting as a memorial of the old burgher
aristocracy, of their character and habits, and of the city in which they
lived ; while to the descendants of the "old gentry" it is interesting as
containing the history of their forefathers and the rise of their families.

GLASGOW—MEMORABILIA OF THE CITY OF GLASGOW Selected from the Minute Books of the Burgh, 1568 to 1750. Fcap. 4to. Half Morocco, Gilt Top. *Very scarce.* 63s.

GLASGOW UNIVERSITY ALBUM FOR THE NEW COLLEGE. With a Photograph of the New College. Edited by Students of the University. Crown 8vo. 7s. 6d.

GLASGOW UNIVERSITY LOCAL EXAMINATIONS. Scheme of Examinations for 1881, and Report for 1880. Crown 8vo. 6d.

GLASGOW UNIVERSITY CALENDAR FOR THE YEAR 1880-81. Published annually. Contains official information as to the University, the Classes, Graduation in all the Faculties, Examination Papers, University Fees, Bursaries, Scholarships and Fellowships, and the list of Members of the General Council of the University. Crown 8vo. 2s.

GOVETT—CHRIST'S RESURRECTION AND OURS ; OR 1. CORINTHIANS XV. EXPOUNDED. By the REV. R. GOVETT, Norwich. Crown 8vo. 3s. 6d.

GRANT—CHRISTIAN BAPTISM EXPLAINED. By the late REV. WILLIAM GRANT, Ayr. 16mo. 1s. 6d.

GRANT—THE LORD'S SUPPER EXPLAINED. By the late REV. WILLIAM GRANT, Ayr. Seventh Edition. 16mo. 4d.

GRAY, David—THE POETICAL WORKS OF DAVID GRAY. Edited by HENRY GLASSFORD BELL, late Sheriff of Lanarkshire. New and enlarged Edition, extra fcap. 8vo. 6s.

" Gems of poetry, exquisitely set."—*Glasgow News.*

JACK—INAUGURAL ADDRESS. Delivered in the University of Glasgow, November 1879. By WILLIAM JACK, M.A., LL.D., Professor of Mathematics in the University of Glasgow. 8vo. 1s.

JEBB—THE ANABASIS OF XENOPHON.—Book III., with the Modern Greek Version of Constantine Bardalachos (for the use of the Greek Classes in the University of Glasgow), and with an Introduction by R. C. JEBB, M.A., Professor of Greek in the University of Glasgow. Crown 8vo. 2s.

LEITCH—PRACTICAL EDUCATIONISTS AND THEIR SYSTEMS OF TEACHING. By JAMES LEITCH, late Principal of the Church of Scotland Normal School, Glasgow. Crown 8vo. 6s.

"This capital book presents us, in a compact and well-digested form, with all that is of most value in the really practical methods of the greatest educationalists."—*School Board Chronicle.*

LEISHMAN—A SYSTEM OF MIDWIFERY, INCLUDING THE DISEASES OF PREGNANCY AND THE PUERPERAL STATE. By WILLIAM LEISHMAN, M.D., Regius Professor of Midwifery in the University of Glasgow. In one Thick Volume. Demy 8vo. Nearly 900 pp., with 210 Wood Engravings. Third Edition, revised. 21s.

"Unquestionably the best modern book on the subject in our language."—*British and Foreign Medico-Chirurgical Review.*
"It is the best English work on the subject."—*Lancet.*
"We should counsel the student by all means to procure Dr. Leishman's work."—*London Medical Record.*
"In many respects not only the best treatise on the subject that we have seen, but one of the best treatises on any medical subject that has been published of late years."—*Practitioner.*

MACELLAR—MEMORIALS OF A MINISTRY ON THE CLYDE. Being Sermons preached in Gourock Free Church. By the late REV. ROBERT MACELLAR. With a Biographical Notice by the REV. A. B. BRUCE, D.D., Professor of Theology, Free Church, Glasgow. With Portrait. Crown 8vo. 7s.

MACEWEN—SERMONS. By the late ALEXANDER MACEWEN, M.A., D.D., Minister of Claremont Church, Glasgow. Edited by his SON. With a Memoir. Crown 8vo. 6s.

MACGEORGE—Papers on the Principles and Real Position of the Free Church. By Andrew Mac-George. 8vo. 6s.

MACLEOD, NORMAN, D.D.—Sermons on the occasion of his Death, preached in the Barony Parish Church, and the Barony Chapel, by the Rev. Dr. Watson, Dundee ; Rev. Dr. Taylor, Crathie ; Rev. Mr. Grant, St. Mary's, Partick ; and Rev. Mr. Morrison, Dunblane. 8vo. 1s.

M'KINLAY, J. Murray—Poems. Extra fcap. 8vo. 3s. 6d.

M'KENDRICK—Outlines of Physiology, in Its Relations to Man. By J. Gray M'Kendrick, M.D., F.R.S.E., Professor of Physiology in the University of Glasgow. Crown 8vo. 750 pages, and 250 Engravings. 12s. 6d.

"We have much pleasure in confidently recommending this work to students of medicine and others, as being the one of all others of recent date, best suited for their requirements."—*British Medical Journal.*

"An admirable book on physiology, well adapted to the wants of the student, and of practitioners in medicine. Such books as this ought to be read, not alone by medical and biological students, but by all men of any pretensions to general culture."—*British Quarterly Review.*

"The style is clear, and the illustrations numerous."—*Practitioner.*

M'KENDRICK—Lectures on the Graphic Method of Physiological Research. Illustrated with numerous Engravings. Crown 8vo. [*In preparation.*

MACMILLAN—Our Lord's Three Raisings from the Dead. By the Rev. Hugh Macmillan, LL.D., F.R.S.E., Author of "Bible Teachings in Nature." Crown 8vo. 6s.

"He has written a book on one of the most trying themes, which is at once edifying and instructive, full of devotional fervour as of fine thought." *Nonconformist.*

"A spirit of earnest piety pervades the book ; its language is simple and unaffected, and it abounds in apt and felicitous illustrations."—*Scotsman.*

MARTYNE—Poems. By Herbert Martyne. Extra fcap. 8vo. 6s.

MAXWELL—ADDRESS TO THE SENATUS AND GENERAL COUNCIL OF THE UNIVERSITY OF GLASGOW. Delivered at his Installation as Chancellor of the University, on the 27th April, 1876. By the late SIR WILLIAM STIRLING MAXWELL, K.T., Bart., M.P. 8vo. 1s.

MORTON—THE TREATMENT OF SPINA BIFIDA BY A NEW METHOD. By JAMES MORTON, M.D., Professor of Materia Medica, Anderson's College, and Surgeon and Clinical Lecturer of Surgery in the Glasgow Royal Infirmary. Crown 8vo. With Six Illustrations. 5s.

MUIR—THE EXPRESSION OF A QUADRATIC SURD AS A CONTINUED FRACTION. By THOMAS MUIR, M.A., F.R.S.E., Examiner in Mathematics in the University of Glasgow. 8vo. 1s. 6d.

MURRAY—OLD CARDROSS, a Lecture. By DAVID MURRAY, M.A., F.S.A. Scot. Crown 8vo, 1s. 6d. Large paper copies, on Dutch Paper, Parchment Wrapper, 6s.

NEWTON—SIR ISAAC NEWTON'S PRINCIPIA. Edited by SIR WILLIAM THOMSON, D.C.L., LL.D., F.R.S., Professor of Natural Philosophy in the University of Glasgow, Fellow of St. Peter's College, Cambridge; and HUGH BLACKBURN, M.A., late Fellow of Trinity College, Cambridge. Crown 4to. 31s. 6d.

" So far as we have compared it with other copies, this edition seems to be better than any of its predecessors. The printing and paper are excellent, and the cuts especially are greatly improved."—*Nature.*

NICHOL—TABLES OF EUROPEAN LITERATURE AND HISTORY, FROM A.D. 200 TO 1876. By JOHN NICHOL, M.A., Balliol, Oxon., LL.D., Regius Professor of English Language and Literature, in the University of Glasgow. 4to, Cloth. 6s. 6d.

" The tables are clear, and form an admirable companion to the student of history, or indeed to any one who desires to revise his recollection of facts."—*Times.*

NICHOL—TABLES OF ANCIENT LITERATURE AND HISTORY, FROM B.C. 1500 TO A.D. 200. By PROFESSOR NICHOL. 4to, Cloth. 4s. 6d.

"They constitute a most successful attempt to give interest to the chronology of literature, by setting before the eye the relation between the literature and the practical life of mankind."—*Observer.*

NICHOL—A NEW VOLUME OF POEMS. [*In preparation.*

OLRIG GRANGE. *See* SMITH.

PORTER—CHRISTIAN PROPHECY : OR POPULAR EXPOSITORY LECTURES ON THE REVELATION TO THE APOSTLE JOHN. By S. T. PORTER. Post 8vo. 7s. 6d.

PORTER—THE LAST SERMONS in a 41 Years' Ministry, and in the 24th Year of Pastorate in the Independent Church, in West Bath Street, Glasgow. By S. T. PORTER. Crown 8vo. 1s. 6d.

PULSFORD—SERMONS PREACHED IN TRINITY CHURCH, GLASGOW. By WILLIAM PULSFORD, D.D. Crown 8vo. Cloth, Red Edges. Cheap Edition. 4s. 6d.

"The sermons have much of the brilliancy of thought and style by which Robertson fascinated his Brighton hearers."—*Daily Review.*
"The preacher we are made to feel, speaks to us out of the fulness of his own spiritual and intellectual life. He is a preacher, because he has been first a thinker."—*Spectator.*

RANKINE—SONGS AND FABLES. By WILLIAM J. MACQUORN RANKINE, late Professor of Engineering in the University of Glasgow. With Portrait, and with Ten Illustrations by J. B. (MRS. HUGH BLACKBURN). Second Edition. Extra fcap. 8vo. 6s.

"These songs are exceedingly bright, strong, and clever : quite the best we have seen for long. They are, in our judgment, far superior to those of Mr. Outram and Lord Neaves, and these are no contemptible singers. An admirable photograph is prefixed to the volume."—*Aberdeen Journal.*

SMITH, Walter C.—RABAN ; OR, LIFE SPLINTERS : a Poem. By the Author of " Olrig Grange." Extra Fcap. 8vo. 7s. 6d.   [*This day.*

SMITH, Walter C.—OLRIG GRANGE : a Poem in Six Books. Edited by HERMANN KUNST, Philol. Professor. Third Edition. Extra fcap. 8vo. 6s. 6d.

" This remarkable poem will at once give its anonymous author a high place among contemporary English poets.—*Examiner.*

" The most sickening phase of our civilization has scarcely been exposed with a surer and quieter point, even by Thackeray himself, than in this advice of a fashionable and religious mother to her daughter."—*Pall Mall Gazette.*

" The pious self-pity of the worldly mother, and the despair of the worldly daughter are really brilliantly put. The story is worked out with quite uncommon power."—*Academy.*

SMITH, Walter C.—BORLAND HALL : a Poem in Six Books. By the Author of " Olrig Grange." Second Edition. Extra fcap. 8vo. 7s.

" Songs of exquisite beauty stud the poem like gems in some massy work of beaten gold. Original and vigorous thought, rare dramatic instinct, and profound knowledge of human nature are embodied in poetry of a very high class. The poem is not only notable in itself, but full of splendid promise."—*Scotsman.*

" Lyell's mother, stern and unrepentant, even in death, is a terrible portrait, in which we recognize the genius of the author of ' Olrig Grange.' . . . A style singularly brilliant and passionately fervent, a verse melodious and various in measure, a command of language, unusually extensive and apt, and an exquisite sensibility to all natural loveliness." —*English Independent.*

SMITH, Walter C.—HILDA ; AMONG THE BROKEN GODS : a Poem. By the Author of " Olrig Grange." Second Edition. Extra fcap. 8vo. 7s. 6d.

" That it is characterized by vigorous thinking, delicate fancy, and happy terms of expression, is admitted on all hands."—*Times.*

" A poem of remarkable power. It contains much fine thought, and shows throughout the deepest penetration into present-day tendencies in belief or no-belief."—*British Quarterly Review.*

SMITH, Walter C.—BISHOP'S WALK ; and Other Poems. Extra fcap 8vo. 2s. 6d.

STANLEY, Dean—THE BURNING BUSH. A Sermon preached before the Glasgow Society of the Sons of Ministers of the Church of Scotland. By the Very Reverend ARTHUR PENRHYN STANLEY, D.D., Dean of Westminster. 8vo. 1s.

STEWART—THE PLAN OF ST. LUKE'S GOSPEL ; A Critical Examination. By the REV. WILLIAM STEWART, M.A., D.D., Regius Professor of Biblical Criticism in Glasgow University. 8vo. 3s. 6d.

STORY—CREED AND CONDUCT : Sermons preached in Rosneath Church. By the REV. ROBERT HERBERT STORY, D.D., Minister of the Parish. Crown 8vo. 7s. 6d.

" Characterized throughout by profound earnestness and spirituality, and written in a style at once graceful, clear, and nervous. Dr. Story has made a well-timed attempt to widen the theology, and at the same time to deepen and intensify the religious feeling of his countrymen."—*Scotsman.*

STORY—ON FAST DAYS ; With reference to more Frequent Communion, and to Good Friday. By the REV. ROBERT HERBERT STORY, D.D., Minister of Rosneath. 8vo. 1s.

"A thoughtful and earnest discussion of a most important question."— *Edinburgh Courant.* " A very able pamphlet."—*Glasgow Herald.*

VEITCH—THE HISTORY AND POETRY OF THE SCOTTISH BORDER, THEIR MAIN FEATURES AND RELATIONS. By JOHN VEITCH, LL.D., Professor of Logic and Rhetoric in the University of Glasgow. Crown 8vo. 10s. 6d.

" This is a genuine book. We can heartily recommend it to three classes of readers—to all who have felt the power of Scott's ' Border Minstrelsy ' (and who with a heart has not ?), to all who care to visit and really to know that delightsome land, for no other book except the ' Border Minstrelsy ' itself will so open their eyes to see it ; to all dwellers in the Borderland who wish to know, as they ought to know, what constitutes the grace and glory of their Borderland."—*Contemporary Review.*
" We feel as if we were hearing the stories, or listening to the snatches of song among the breezes of the mountains or the moorland, under the sun-broken mists of the wild glens, or the wooded banks of the Yarrow or the Tweed."—*Times.*
" The fullest, most thorough, and most deeply critical work on Border history and poetry that we have."—*British Quarterly Review.*

VEITCH—LUCRETIUS AND THE ATOMIC THEORY. By PRO-
FESSOR VEITCH.   Crown 8vo.   3s. 6d.

" We have read this little volume with no ordinary delight.   We warmly
recommend it."—*Nonconformist.*

VEITCH—HILLSIDE RHYMES :

" Among the rocks he went,
And still looked up to sun and cloud
And listened to the wind."

Extra fcap. 8vo.   5s.

" Let any one who cares for fine reflective poetry read for himself and
judge.   Next to an autumn day among the hills themselves, commend us
to poems like these, in which so much of the finer breath and spirit of those
pathetic hills is distilled into melody."—*Scotsman.*

VEITCH—THE TWEED, AND OTHER POEMS.   Extra fcap. 8vo.
6s. 6d.

" Every page bears witness to a highly cultivated mind : every page is
also marked by originality and a deep love for nature."—*Westminster
Review.*

VILLAGE LIFE—A Poem.

" He seems to be a stranger ; but his present is
A withered branch, that's only green at top."

Extra fcap 8vo.   6s. 6d.

" These are simply the ripest notes that have appeared in Scotland for
a time too long to calculate."—*Examiner.*
" A remarkable volume of poetry, which will be read by all who have
any keen interest in the progress of English literature."—*Standard.*

WADDELL—OSSIAN AND THE CLYDE, FINGAL IN IRELAND,
OSCAR IN ICELAND ; or, Ossian Historical and Authentic.
By P. HATELY WADDELL, LL.D.   4to.   12s. 6d.

WATSON—KANT AND HIS ENGLISH CRITICS, a comparison
of Critical and Empirical Philosophy.   By JOHN WATSON,
M.A., LL.D., Professor of Moral Philosophy in Queen's
University, Kingston, Canada.   8vo.   [*In the Press.*

.

www.ingramcontent.com/pod-product-compliance
Lightning Source LLC
Chambersburg PA
CBHW020338030726
47496CB00007B/1939